RED ROCK RENEGADES

When the South-Western Detective
Agency took on the Strang case,
Slim Blake believed that the outlaw
Willie Marvin was alive. On a search
for Willie he took a beating before
leaving for New Mexico to contact
the new client. Jason Strang often
had tricksters after his money, but
Edith Lamont was a 'grafter'.
Working on the plot against Jason,
Slim's life was endangered. Willie
Marvin and his kidnappers had to
be fought with bullets and guile in
Red Rock Canyon before Jason
could resume his ordinary way of
life.

DAVID BINGLEY

RED ROCK RENEGADES

Complete and Unabridged

LINFORD
Leicester

First published in Great Britain in 1970

First Linford Edition
published 2006

British Library CIP Data

Bingley, David
  Red Rock renegades.—Large print ed.—
Linford western library
  1. Western stories
  2. Large type books
  I. Title
  823.9'14 [F]

  ISBN 1–84617–127–X

Published by
F. A. Thorpe (Publishing)
Anstey, Leicestershire

Set by Words & Graphics Ltd.
Anstey, Leicestershire
Printed and bound in Great Britain by
T. J. International Ltd., Padstow, Cornwall

This book is printed on acid-free paper

1

The hands on the big dusty-faced clock in the square of the town of Amarillo, North Texas, showed that the day had progressed to the second hour of the afternoon. The town was a big, sprawling prosperous settlement, steadily booming through the influence of the railroad, but at that time of the day it was relatively quiet.

The lean, thoughtful young rider on the back of the spritely dun quarter horse was positively the only saddle traveller moving on Main Street as he came down from the direction of the railroad track and angled his mount towards a two-storey office with a creaking shingle swinging from the wall at the upper level.

Jim Blake, known as 'Slim' because of his sparely-built muscular figure, peered up at the shingle, his intense blue eyes narrowed under the bent brim of the flat dun stetson which protected his head from the heat of the sun.

He massaged his tapering sideburns which were fair with a hint of sandy colour in them. His mouth quirked into a crooked ingenuous smile as he read the words on the shingle. He patted imaginary dust out of the grey leather vest which hung loosely over his faded blue shirt.

The notice said: *South-Western Detective Agency. Proprietor: Horace Danson. Inquire within.*

Half to himself and half to the horse, he murmured: 'Doggone it, here we are again, all set for an interrogation with the Boss. An' where will it get me, I wonder?'

He did not deign to answer his own question, but tethered the dun to the hitch rail and solemnly slackened the saddle. After patting the horse lightly on the rump, he moved silently up onto the sidewalk, crossed to the office door and entered the building. There was a smell of dust in the air of the hall which always made him wish he was elsewhere. Through the door to the left was the general office, usually occupied by a rather faded female clerk, Bella Marr. The door on the other side, with the frosted glass panel, gave access to the private office of Horace Danson himself.

Slim hesitated, but finally decided to announce himself directly to the Boss. He listened, heard a faint wheezing snore coming from inside the room, and silently turned the door knob. Danson was in the comfortably padded armchair behind the glass-topped desk.

The newcomer eyed him speculatively for a few seconds before crossing on silent feet to stand beside the sleeper. A slight tendency towards mischievous practical joking made Slim fish a small coin out of his pocket and roll it between his fingers.

Danson, a stout man in a checked buttoned vest topped by a grey suit, slumbered on with his ample jowl hidden under a shiny black stetson which had been planted on his face. Bending closer, Slim placed the coin against the side of the sleeper's neck and awaited a reaction.

In his sleep, Danson tensed, quivered and gripped the arms of the chair. His eyes, most likely, had opened under the hat, but he hesitated to make any other kind of move without permission.

Speaking in a lower tone than normal, Slim murmured: 'Now take it real easy, amigo, an' then nothing untoward will happen to you!'

Danson groaned, shifted his grip on the chair, but did nothing else. He was rapidly coming wide awake, and was fearful of what lay ahead of him. Almost a minute passed with the tension still unrelieved. Eventually, Slim's muted chuckle gave Danson the idea that the circle of metal on his neck might not after all be a gun muzzle. The frightened man took a few more seconds to muster his courage before whipping the hat off his face and challenging his persecutor.

'Slim, you fool! What in tarnation's gotten into you? Don't you know a trick like that could stop a man's heart?'

Danson fell to massaging his chest, and this made Slim feel a little guilty. The younger man parked his hip on the end of the desk and took off his hat. He could apologise most feelingly when he wanted, but Danson, who knew this, waved him into silence. The proprietor glanced at his pocket watch, snorted and reassembled himself in the chair, fumbling a small cigar out of his vest pocket.

'Ain't no wonder I fell asleep waitin' for you, you young varmint! You were due in off the Limited, and that went through several hours ago! So where have you been occupyin' your time since then, or shouldn't I ask?'

Slim, who was working on his face with a red bandanna, showed mild annoyance as he prepared to explain the delay.

'All right, don't bother,' Danson went

on, 'you've been on the hunt for Willie Marvin since you got back from Dumas. Chasin' that dead or alive hero is becomin' an obsession with you, boy. But let me ask you, did you finish the Dale case with the Dumas people?'

Slim brightened a little. 'Oh, sure, the thief took the stuff I'd planted. He's in jail now. I talked with the marshal, the mayor and the traveller who had previously lost his property. The Dumas affair is all tied up. But to get back to Willie Marvin.'

The young man paused for a moment, rasping his thumb along his normally smooth chin. He looked up while Danson waited, and his expression hardened.

'I know you don't believe Willie Marvin is still alive. Jest the same, I swear I saw him that time over towards the New Mexico border. So don't scoff too hard, Horace. I haven't found Willie, but certain information which I've picked up since my return keeps his case quite interesting.'

Danson sighed, yawned, massaged his rubbery jowl and raised his sparse eyebrows. His fat lips closed on the end of the cigar. He talked around it.

'All right, so tell me the latest, but make it brief because I ain't sittin' here jest to make you welcome. I've got work for you.'

Slim shrugged, but went on. 'Willie is supposed to be buried at Bitter Springs jest east of here. Right? Well, I'm still sayin' he ain't in the coffin they have buried in the extension to Bitter Springs' Boot Hill! Right now there's a rumour goin' around that his mother — Willie's mother — is trying to get the coffin lifted and sent to where she resides, in Kansas. What do you think to that?'

Danson spat out a sliver of tobacco. He did not appear to be particularly impressed about the latest news about the notorious young renegade who so interested Slim. 'What about it, any-ways? Even the mother of an outlaw is entitled to some feelings after her boy has died. This thing that you have learned don't have to be significant at all!'

'It could be, though,' Slim insisted. He leaned forward and gestured towards his Boss with a spatulate forefinger. 'If that wooden coffin was the hidin' place for loot which has been missin' since Willie's owlhoot buddies split up, this could be an attempt to get the funds back into circulation. Anyway, I'd like the opportunity to keep a watch on what happens to the coffin in the next day or so, if you feel you can give me permission.'

Slim leaned back and pulled a tobacco sack out of the pocket of his shirt. His blue eyes were watching Danson's expression very closely. Danson knew this, and he made no attempt to sweeten his countenance.

'I have this job lined up for you. One which would put your persistence and energy to the test,' Danson explained. 'Moreover, it ain't in these parts, an' if you took it maybe this obsession about

Willie Marvin might be broken. I can see by your face you ain't really listenin' to what I'm sayin'.'

In order to give the lie to Danson's words, Slim replied: 'Couldn't Ron take the job on?'

He was referring to Ron McCartney, an older and perhaps steadier detective, who shared the enquiry work with Slim. Almost at once, Danson began to shake his head.

'Nope. Ron is already workin' on a ranch job, an' there's another one comin' up very shortly. He's good at sortin' out ranchers' wrangles, an' there I intend to keep him.' After a short silence, the stout man looked up and glared at Slim and the smoke he was in the act of lighting. 'I'll tell you what I'll do, Slim. You can have twenty-four hours to look further into this matter at Bitter Springs. After that, barrin' any startlin' development, you'll be startin' on the new job an' there'll be no puttin' the matter off any longer. Savvy?'

Slim nodded. He rolled his cigarette

around his mouth and grinned appreciatively. 'Okay, Horace, I'll do as you say. You made a pretty fair decision. I know you ain't givin' me this time because you figure things the way *I* do, but you'll blush jest the same if I turn up little Willie in the land of the livin'.'

He rose to his feet and made for the door, spinning his weathered hat on an index finger. Danson nodded and watched him go. The proprietor wondered once again if there was any truth in Slim's belief that Willie Marvin lived. Within ten minutes, sleep began to make Danson's eyelids heavy once again.

★   ★   ★

Bitter Springs was a smaller settlement roughly three miles east of Amarillo and on slightly higher ground.

Slim Blake deliberately kept away from it until the light was fading that evening. He made a small detour to avoid the light spilling out into the streets from the houses and the places of pleasure. He knew the town well, as it was so close to his base, and he found a place in which to watch the annexe to the main cemetery without any difficulty.

Having assured himself that no one else was paying particular attention to the graveyard, he took his mount into a slim stand of timber about one hundred yards away, and pegged it out. An observer would have been interested to note that he took with him to his lookout spot his Winchester and a spyglass, as well as the .45 Colt strapped to the right side of his body.

Slim really believed that Marvin lived, and that there was some unexplained mystery about the coffin said to contain his remains. If an attempt was being made to remove the coffin, that did not mean that Willie was likely to be in the area; but it could mean that his old associates might be hanging about. Slim had given the whole affair a lot of thought, and because he thought renegades might attempt to remove the coffin without waiting for the proper authority, he had come along late at night to keep a private vigil.

Squatting unobtrusively behind a low stone wall, he soon found that his eyes were playing tricks with him in the gathering darkness. He blinked them a lot, and from time to time put the glass to his eye to peer around him at a distance. In the direction of the town, soft lamplight showed in patches, but no one came away from the streets to join him.

An hour had gone by when he began to relax his vigilance and wonder what sort of a job Horace had lined up for him. All he knew about it was that it was likely to prove difficult, and that it was at some distance from Amarillo County. Many thoughts went slowly through his head. He was wondering what it would be like to do inquiry work exclusively connected with missing persons when a whispered exclamation carried to his straining ears.

A human noise followed the whisper, as though someone who was cautious, or out of breath, was answering. Three minutes went by before he heard the first definite sound of a boot on small loose stones. Someone was coming in his direction, towards the burial ground. Perhaps, after all, his vigil was not to be in vain. His heart thumped with excitement at the possible prospect of action by night.

About twenty yards away, the voices seemed to stop advancing. A hoarse voice said: 'If you ask me, Ross, this little jaunt is unnecessary. Jest at a time when we're here to persuade the authorities to have the coffin raised, I'd say it was foolish to come along here an' risk bein' caught diggin'. Why the sudden change of plan?'

'It's one thing to ask for a coffin to be raised, an' another thing to be granted permission. Especially as the corpse was a wanted outlaw. You wouldn't want to leave here empty-handed, any more than *I* would. So take my advice.

I've dealt with coroners an' undertakers before today, so help me.'

Slim was smiling in the darkness. He was thinking of shifting his position to get a better view of the two conspirators when a faint sound came in his direction. It was almost like that created on a still night by a hostile Indian arrow. He had long enough to know a few seconds of disquiet, and then something heavy hit the back of his head and slowly robbed him of his consciousness.

2

His buckled hat brim had given under the weight of the missile, leaving the stetson still sitting rather unevenly on his head. Noises appeared to be magnified in his ears as the men he had heard hurried towards the spot.

He fought with his ebbing consciousness for several seconds, although he knew he must lose the battle. He was on his knees and almost rolling earthwards when the two conspirators leapt the wall and came down almost on top of him.

'Will you look at this? We've gotten ourselves a snooper! Maybe we ought to teach him a lesson.'

Other sounds suggested that a third man was coming from another direction. Slim had sufficient clarity of mind to know that this third man might have been the one to throw the missile. After that, his thoughts swept through his head at a sickening speed and ceased to make sense.

'Hey, there's a horse up there in the trees,' the second voice murmured.

'It figures,' the third arrival gasped. 'It was the hoss gave me the idea we weren't alone. Maybe it was a good thing I came along by a different route.'

Slim no longer heard as his fate was decided.

'We ought to teach this hombre a lesson, boys,' the most authoritative voice suggested.

'Wouldn't it be better to do what we came to do first? We could deal with him later,' the third man argued.

Number Two, who had a cruel streak, warmed to the idea of making an example of the man who had spied on the burial ground. 'No, let's act on Ross's suggestion,' he put in warmly. 'After all, if the authorities refuse to give permission to lift the coffin we can do it another night.'

Before his partners could offer any

substantial protest, the man with the least control aimed a kick in Slim's side which made him feel the pain in spite of his semiconsciousness. The victim groaned. The first persecutor kicked him on the thigh, and then, seemingly with a touch of reluctance, the other two joined in.

Weighty kicks and punches sank into Slim's body, sending shooting pains into his guts, his head and his chest. One of the trio had damaged other men before, and he appeared to take a delight in what he was doing. Some three minutes later, the beating came to an end when the man giving the instructions sent the sadistic man away to collect the startled dun.

★　★　★

At eight o'clock in the morning, Whiskers Gannon, long-term head barman of the Broken Wheel saloon in Bitter Springs, came out from the front of the establishment where he worked and carried a box full of empty bottles into the alley beside it.

The bruised and bloody body which attempted to rise from behind the second of the three trash cans gave him a shock which set his fatted heart racing. Whiskers was a rotund, cylindrical man, whose stocky body was well wrapped in a white apron of voluminous proportions. He deposited the bottles on the ground beside the cans, and stepped back a pace the better to see the fellow on the ground.

Two cuts and a slightly blackened eye made it hard for the barman to study the features, but he felt sure that this man was not one of those who had been imbibing in the saloon on the previous evening. He was not a regular visitor to the Broken Wheel, though Whiskers thought he had seen him before.

Slim Blake, for it was he, blinked his eyes and gestured for assistance, but the barman, who was allergic to bloodshed, stepped back still further and went away to where the end of the alley came up with the dirt of the street. Few people were about on the street, but Gannon's expression relaxed when he saw the two-horse buckboard of Sam Trevor, the town's able though ageing doctor.

'Hey, Doc,' he called, 'could you spare a minute? There's a man back there in the alley who could do with a bit of attention from you.'

Trevor, a tall, almost gaunt man in his late fifties, hauled on his reins and halted his conveyance. He was just about to start his round of out-of-town calls and not keen to be stopped at this juncture. Moreover, he did not approve of men who got themselves into a state through imbibing too much liquor, and he felt sure that the man who required his help was such a case.

Leaving his buckboard for a moment, Trevor moved into the alley and put a hand to his rounded back while he bent over the stricken figure and studied his condition. The injured man smelled strongly of liquor, but Trevor was sufficiently wide awake to know that the smell did not come from his lips. This he confirmed by holding up the head, and tilting it back.

Slim managed a weak smile. 'Howdy, Doc? It sure is good to see you. Could you smuggle me away from this garbage an' patch me up a little? I seem to have run into a little opposition.'

'I know you now. You're young Slim Blake, that detective's man from Amarillo. I suppose you'll tell me that you didn't go on a drinkin' spree last night an' expect me to believe you!'

'You suggested there might be some doubt about it, Doc, not me,' Slim pointed out.

Trevor offered him a rather weak shoulder and called out sharply for Gannon to come and help. Between them they managed to lower Slim onto the rear portion of the buckboard, and no one in the vicinity was any the wiser for their action.

'Keep this matter to yourself, Whiskers,' the doctor ordered tersely.

He knew how talkative the barman was, particularly when his tongue had been loosened by liquor. Gannon nodded rather sheepishly, and retired indoors with a thoughtful expression on his face.

★ ★ ★

Ten minutes later, Slim was stretched out on the couch in Trevor's surgery with his shirt off. The doctor was making a thorough examination of all his cuts and bruises with a view to checking for actual breakages as well as for contusions.

As he continued the examination, the nimble-fingered sawbones gave a murmured recital of his finds, which did nothing to restore Slim's confidence. There were two short cuts on the head: one behind an ear and the other higher on the crown. His right cheekbone was swollen; there was a lump under his left eye. The rib cage revealed three more discoloured bruises, and two other ugly patches showed, one on his hip and the other on a thigh.

Trevor bathed and dressed the contusions, one after another. His bright, bird-like eyes were often on the young man's face. He did more than study Slim's capacity for absorbing pain. He was genuinely curious as to how the blows had been administered, and what Slim had done to acquire them.

In order to give his thoughts reasonable activity, Slim decided to reveal something of the happening. 'I was up at Boot Hill, shortly after dark last night, when a group of three men jumped me. One of them threw something which hit me on the back of the head, otherwise this would not have happened.

'The whisky was added to my clothing some time later. They made an example of me so that others wouldn't go snooping around the burial ground.'

Trevor took time out to stroke the small tuft of grey beard on his chin. He was more thoughtful than ever when he replied. 'Some years ago, students in my profession got themselves a bad name through stealin' the bodies of the dead so that practisin' surgeons could cut them up and learn about men's innards. I don't suppose you were up to anything like that, though keepin' watch on a graveyard sounds highly improper whoever makes the suggestion.'

After a short pause, Slim explained. 'I'm interested in the coffin which is supposed to house the body of Willie Marvin. I thought interested parties might try to dig it up and go off with it when no one was around. I heard enough to make me sure that something strange was goin' on. But do go easy with that cleansin' solution, Doc, it's burnin' me like acid!'

Trevor laughed rather grimly. He had taken in the substance of Slim's disclosure, but he declined to remark on it. Soon, he had finished ministering to his patient, other than the head cuts. In order to facilitate the healing of these, he produced an open-bladed razor and trimmed close the hair on and around the cuts. Slim waited patiently for him to be finished.

'Seein' as how you were on important work when your setback occurred, I'm only chargin' a nominal fee. Give me a dollar,' Trevor suggested. 'If you take my advice, you'll stay here an' rest for an hour or two before you return to that stout Boss of yours an' tell him what has happened to you.'

Slim made as if to get up, but the doctor pushed him back again.

'Stay where you are, son. You can make yourself some coffee in the kitchen when you've had an hour or two of proper rest. If you're bothered about your horse, I'll have the livery-man's boy seek it out an' bring it round to the hitchrail. Will you do as I say?'

Slim nodded. He parted with a silver

dollar and looked away, while the doctor made his preparations for the second time that morning.

*   *   *

The sun was past its zenith again when Slim rode the dun towards Danson's office to report. The rider was glad of the heat for once. It had driven many people off the streets and that meant that there were few to see his battered condition.

The smell of coffee greeted him as he went in, but that did not prevent Danson sniffing when he smelled the odour of whisky, which still clung to the young detective's clothing.

Danson looked surprised, but by no means dumbfounded. 'Pull up a chair an' take a cup of coffee with me,' he offered.

Slim complied, quickly and gratefully. He sipped it through battered lips which pained him slightly due to the heat. 'Somebody got through to me while I was watchin' by the graveyard late last night.'

'I can see they did, Slim. What happened to you probably means that there's something goin' on back there which is not altogether lawful. But be that as it may, it ain't the business of this detective agency.'

'Are you sayin' that you are sendin' me on a new job before you've heard what I have to say?'

Danson gave him a long, hard, baleful glance. 'I mean jest that, my boy. If it's any consolation to you, the permission to dig up the coffin has been refused. And there my own and your interest must rest. If I can't get through to you about this new case, I'm finished with you, Jim Blake, an' that's plain Western talk. So if you're goin' to protest, do it now!'

The proprietor lowered his eyes to the desk top, and waited, as though he was anticipating trouble.

'You are sayin' I'm finished with the agency, that I have to take my pay an'

26

go elsewhere, if I don't go on this new job?' Slim asked.

'That's exactly the case, young fellow, so do you still work for me, or don't you?'

'I still need work,' Slim admitted, with a forced smile which pained him. 'So perhaps you'd better tell me the details. But I'll never be able to get out of my mind that I'm runnin' away from trouble, goin' off on this other job.'

'Maybe you'll come to terms with yourself if the new job happens to be tougher, Slim. So listen good, 'cause I don't have a lot of time for explanations. You're a good reader, an' you spend time lookin' through the newspapers. Do you ever come across the *Las Vegas Chronicle*?'

Slim frowned. He fingered his hurt face and then nodded. 'Sure, I've seen it. A weekly paper published in New Mexico territory, presumably in Las Vegas. Why, what's it got to do with the case?'

'I thought maybe you might have

noticed the name of a man who often writes for it these days. Jason Strang. He's a former rancher who dabbles in all sorts of subjects an' writes about them. Does the name mean anything to you?'

Slim was nodding again. 'Sure, I've seen the name and some of his work. He's knowledgeable about cattle, and recent history, an' also about some rather unusual subjects, such as diet. What people eat, in towns and out of towns, and how they're affected in war.'

Danson produced a small bent cigar from his pocket and carefully straightened it. 'Jason Strang is in trouble,' he said, his voice scarcely above a murmur.

'You want me to go to Las Vegas to give Jason Strang some sort of protection, Horace?'

'That's what I expect of you, Slim. I can give you a few details. First off, this ain't any sort of run-of-the-mill guard duty, even if it's soundin' that way. You see, Jason Strang ain't an old man, although he's retired from ranchin'. As a matter of fact, he's no more than forty, which makes him years younger than — than me, for instance.

'He ain't noted for his good looks, as far as I know, but he has a mighty attractive appeal to some people. He has a lot of money. A self-made man, who this far has not spent any of his gains on anyone. A bachelor, and very eligible.'

Slim rocked forward in his chair and pointed with his forefinger, a gesture which was becoming a habit. 'I seem to recollect Strang havin' written an article about pistol shootin', so how come he needs a man like me to straighten out his affairs?'

'Didn't I jest say it wasn't jest a guard job?' Danson complained. 'Somebody is gettin' through to Strang, gettin' after his money. He's been fendin' off get-rich-quick shysters for upwards of ten years, but right now he has a real problem. Somebody with a new angle for takin' his money, an' he sure is troubled. We're lucky because he wanted a detective whose face was not known in the district around where he lives. Here's hopin' all them cuts are healed before you get there, otherwise you'll soon become known, an' that'll finish you as far as this case is concerned.'

Slim glowered. 'I'll have you know my flesh is quick healin' an' that none of these cuts will show by the time I get there. When do I start out?'

Danson examined the question, in the light of other things which he had in mind. 'Seein' as how you've been roughed up a little, I'm givin' you permission to stay in town until early tomorrow, but if you so much as set foot in the direction of Bitter Springs, so help me I'll disown you, an' you'll have to come an' beg for your pay.'

Slim sniffed. He rose to his feet, but did not grumble. 'If you're in a calm frame of mind, I'll see you in the Chinaman's place around the usual time for dinner. Okay?'

Danson agreed without enthusiasm. Slim walked out looking thoughtful. He was wondering where in town he could get his hands on back numbers of the *Las Vegas Chronicle.*

3

A week later, two scarcely honest drifters were seeking a man who had gone to earth on a little frequented trail between Las Vegas and the smaller town of San Juan in a north-eastern county of New Mexico territory. For forty-eight hours the pair had been living it up in the latter town on the proceeds of a walk-in robbery at a farm set well away from its neighbours.

The previous night they had run out of credit and of funds, and now, through rolling a lone traveller on the trail, they sought to replenish their vanished funds.

Shamus Hughes, the older of the two, was a balding, beefy man in badly worn corduroy trail clothes. He had bloodshot eyes which gave away his main weakness in life. The pinto under him was hard-ridden, like the roan which carried his partner, Tammy Dowell. Dowell was a taller, slightly younger man with a thick nose and close-set eyes. His thick black hair contrasted in the brows and sideburns with a prison pallor which no amount of sun appeared to affect.

'I tell you he didn't see you, nor me either,' Shamus was arguing. 'So there has to be a reason why he's given up riding an' gone to earth!'

'I'll grant you that, Shamus, my friends, but let's not underestimate him. A man was tellin' me back there in town he's the famous Jason Strang, a wealthy man and a writer of articles for the newspapers. The man who told me said Strang was a very shrewd person, and that's a fact.'

Hughes hauled round the head of his horse. 'Well, I say he's hunkered down within a furlong of this spot, an' if we want any of his ready money we've got to find him before he hears your tongue waggin'!'

Dowell chuckled, not having listened

to the last rebuke. 'A man who travels around like that, one who owned a ranch and then sold it, he'd carry quite a few dollars in his bill fold, wouldn't he, Shamus?'

'Shut your face, an' follow me close, will you? I'm listenin' an' so is the hoss, if you'll give it a chance!'

Dowell, still not daunted, rubbed his thick nose and continued to speculate. 'He piled up his wealth in cattle ranchin', so I've been told. What I'm slow to understand is why somebody hasn't managed to take his money away from him before this. Do you have any ideas on the subject?'

'I do an' all!' Hughes retorted. 'I'd say most of the folks who fancied his money let their tongues run away with them!'

This time Dowell laughed fitfully, and became quite thoughtful in the silence which grew between them after that. He was thinking that their victim was making it all too easy for them. Other men, even if they were simply out of town for a little horse-riding exercise, would stick to the beaten tracks. This route they were on looked as if the last creature to use it was a bear, and that was none too recent. Why would a man of means ride off the beaten track and go to earth in a stunted belt of trees?

Hughes held up a horny hand on which were five well-chewed nails. As Dowell came level with him, he glanced at him sideways, as though speculating as to whether his partner was prepared to listen to him.

Dowell waited, and presently Hughes talked. 'If you ask me, he has to be in that stand of timber right ahead of us. Jest in case he's wise to us, maybe we ought to make the approach from two directions at once.'

'We dismount, then, and creep up on him?' Dowell suggested.

Hughes nodded very deliberately. He pointed away to his right, where a slight hollow afforded useful cover for their horses. A minute later, they had swung out of leather and walked the animals down the slope. When they were ready to move, the older man wiped his sweating hands down the worn cord of his jacket.

'I could do with a smoke before we go after him,' he murmured, 'but we don't have the makings, so that will have to wait.'

'He could have tobacco on him, cigars even,' Dowell murmured optimistically, 'so why don't we make a start? The sooner we've done the job, the better.'

Hughes managed a wolfish grin. He then indicated the direction from which he intended to make his approach, and indicated a suggested route for his partner. They parted almost at once, and entered upon a period of extreme caution in movement.

* * *

Even on his back, with a chewed wooden pencil between his teeth, Jason Strang was a striking figure. His soft, black, expensive felt stetson, worn undented, was pushed forward over his forehead to keep the sun out of his eyes. As he chewed the pencil, the slight movement of his facial muscles rocked the thick black moustache which hung in a drooping arc from the outer sides of his upper lip. His long, pointed jaw partially hid the maroon cravat and diamond stick-pin at his throat. A well-cut grey suit hid the slight thickening of his body at the waist.

Beside him lay a small paper pad, and a gun belt and holster which held a .45 Colt and the requisite ammunition. The grey eyes, which could reveal so much of his character and mood, on this occasion merely showed a fierce concentration, as Strang stared up through the leafy branches between himself and the sun.

He had practised the use of the simple everyday language favoured in Western newspapers for quite a time. Now he was indulging himself in another form of writing — one which did not come quite so easily. He was attempting to compose a few verses of poetry about the effects of the brassy sun upon animals, birds and humans in that part of the West. His composing was a slow labour, which never seemed to get any easier.

His ears, however, were keenly attuned to local sounds, and, some five minutes after his two would-be attackers had parted company, he began to be aware of tiny sounds coming from two directions. A man not used to the open air might have failed to detect the approach of humans, but not so Jason Strang.

His expression changed from one of frustration over the difficulty of his self-imposed task to one of interest and anticipation of the coming clash. He could have written a book about the many ways in which men and women attempted to separate him from his ample funds. Some were subtle; others were blatantly obvious. He had ridden out of town to try and distract himself from one worrying form of approach. In a way, it was a relief to have to cope with this rather elementary form of bushwhacking.

He yawned rather loudly, shifted his position so that it was comfortable to prop his head upon an elbow, extracted a small cigar from his inside pocket, and proceeded to light it, one handed. When his nostrils were giving out the smoke in twin jets, he drove the burning end of the match into the soil, thus extinguishing it. His free hand then wandered around his throat area and extracted from a secret pocket sewn into the rear side of the cravat a small but very effective two-shot Derringer pistol. This he palmed and laid against his chest.

He appeared to be in a deep reverie, but from that moment nothing escaped him: no sounds, and no movement.

★ ★ ★

Hughes had chosen for himself the shortest route to the victim. He it was who cautiously doffed his hat some fifteen yard away and prepared to make the last rush on foot, through the lush grass. Dowell had signalled two minutes earlier, and Hughes, who was certain of an easy 'kill', wanted to be the first on the spot so that he could appropriate Strang's stock of cigars.

The bald attacker rose to his feet, a Colt in his right fist. He paused for a mere second or so, and then started forward with the minimum of noise. He had advanced by about three yards when his bloodshot eyes opened wide in surprise. The victim had suddenly come to life. A small gun which was almost concealed in the palm of his hand was pointed in Hughes' direction, and the face behind it showed that Strang had clearly understood and interpreted their intentions.

Before the attacker could level his gun, or protest, the tiny Derringer had been fired. A small puff of smoke followed from Strang's hand, while the bullet burned the tip of Hughes' right ear. Hughes pulled up quite suddenly, hesitated about firing back, and received a shallow but telling burn along the left side of his chest.

Emitting a cry of surprise, mingled with a bit extra for shooting pains, Hughes lunged backwards, lost his footing, staggered, recovered and threw himself down. All he wanted at that moment was to be out of Strang's line of fire. The victim had already turned his attention away from the first attacker. Moving with the speed of a striking snake, he had thrown himself sideways and snatched up the gun belt.

With the .45 in his fist, he bounded to his feet, ran three yards and dived into longer grass in the direction of his second attacker. Dowell, knowing his partner had been discomfited, fired off two revolver bullets which went close.

Undeterred, Strang braced his shoulders and began to fire steadily at the tree which hid the second man.

Dowell's hat left his head and flew into sight from behind the bole. As bullets continued to chip wood near to his head, Dowell gave up. He slipped to the ground and began to wriggle away from the scene of the exchanges as fast as he was able.

A minute went by before Strang realised this. In that time Hughes might have caught him at a disadvantage, but Shamus had no heart for an attack on a man with so much fire in his belly. One shot from the Strang weapon was sufficient to send him back in the direction by which he had arrived.

Strang was pleased with himself. Still moving cautiously, he made good time over the nearest route to where he supposed the attackers had left their horses. He was a little bit out in his calculations. As a result, Hughes was able to shoo the animals in a direction which made it easier for them to mount up without stopping a bullet.

Strang's parting shots, however, went very close. One of them burned

Dowell's shoulder as he threw himself into the saddle. As the retreating ruffians went out of view, Strang selected a tree bole and leaned against it. He sucked steadily on his cigar, watching the growth of the ash on the end of it. The excitement had improved his spirits.

He began to reflect that positive action had, for him, more of an attraction than painful creative endeavour.

★ ★ ★

It was coincidental that Slim Blake was, at that same time, within the sound of gunfire, on the trail between Las Vegas and San Juan. He had spent the best part of three days travelling westward into New Mexico territory by railroad, and since then the dun had worked hard under him to bring him to Las Vegas in less than seven days.

In Las Vegas he had been informed that his contact lived in the smaller settlement of San Juan. Consequently, towards midday on that particular day, he was riding towards San Juan in the hope of meeting up with Strang on arrival.

The two Derringer shots had scarcely carried to him, but the discharges of the heavier weapons had reverberated across the intervening ground and convinced him that someone way off the usual track was in trouble. He arrived in the area of the shooting some five minutes after the attackers had left it.

The lack of humans made him rein in within a short distance of the man he sought. He was beginning to think that he had come too late, or that he had made a mistake, when he caught a distant glimpse of a fine-looking smoke-grey stallion which appeared to be eaten up with curiosity.

Its sudden appearance on the far side of a hill slope drew Slim nearer. He was within twenty yards of it when he noticed for the first time that an alert, well-dressed stranger was pacing up the slope behind him with a smoking weapon held muzzle downwards in his right hand. The interest in the stallion faded. Slim checked the dun, cautiously slipped to the ground and regarded the newcomer over his saddle.

Strang continued to come nearer. At almost every footfall, he sucked on his cigar. To Slim he looked to be doing all his breathing through the weed. His approach and manner merited caution, which Slim certainly showed him. The young detective decided to try a friendly approach.

'Howdy, stranger. I came off the trail because I heard gun shots. I thought somebody over in this direction might be in a little trouble, but you don't look like a man in a tight situation.'

Strang continued to be watchful, but he was already forming a favourable opinion of Slim.

'Trouble surely was aimed at me, young fellow. Let's say I managed to cope with it. Did you see a couple of hard-ridin' desperate men hittin' the trail at all in the last few minutes?'

Slim shook his head and grinned. 'Maybe they were movin' too fast for the human eye to detect them, or something. Me, I have business in San Juan, but if there is anything I can do I'll be glad to help.'

'Wait till I collect my horse and another item an' I'll ride along with you,' Strang suggested. 'It was good of you to come over here an' try to help.'

At this point, he turned his back on Slim, as though he trusted him fully. The young detective walked the dun up the slope and admired the well-muscled stallion which came as its master whistled. Strang abandoned the animal long enough for him to retrieve his pencil, the empty Derringer and the notebook. He came back, thrusting the latter into his side pocket and offered Slim his hand.

'How are you, young fellow? I'm Jason Strang. I have a house in San Juan.'

Slim partook of a warm handshake, but he was slow to give his own name. He was grinning broadly about the way in which he had met his principal, by chance. Strang started to shake his head.

'You ain't that young detective fellow I've been expecting, Jim Blake, are you? On the way in from Amarillo, Texas?'

'That's me, Mr Strang. Sent by my Boss, Horace Danson. I must admit I wasn't keen to come at first, but now that I've met you I can see that this assignment ain't likely to be a dull one. I wish I'd been a bit sooner, and then I could have helped you drive off your attackers. I presume whoever it was wanted whatever money you were carrying?'

'I guess so, Jim. But no harm was done. They were easy to deal with. Most of the folks after the Strang money can be dealt with, provided care is taken. I say most. For the first time since I became widely known through my work in the papers, I'm beginning to think that clever people can do me harm. I'm under some pressure from out of town. That's why I sent for help from a detective agency whose operatives are not known around him. You've come a long way, but I might have to ask you to travel some more. How do you feel about that?'

Slim mounted up before answering. He patted the mane of the sweating dun and looked it over for any signs of strain.

'Travellin' is all part of the job, Mr Strang. I'll take whatever is comin' to me on this assignment, though I'd appreciate a little time for my horse to rest up. Would I be right in thinking some big outlaw outfit is puttin' pressure on you?'

Strang mounted up with quiet deliberation. He pushed back his hat, and massaged his brow, which was furrowed. 'If you mean outlaws in the sense of folks actin' outside the law, I suppose that could be the case. But I figure you'll be surprised to know that the main threat this time is comin' from a woman!'

Slim whistled in sudden surprise. In nearly all the cases he had worked on for Danson's agency, the crooks and law-breakers had been almost exclusively men. For the first time it occurred to him that the Strang case might be very different from his past experience.

4

The ride into San Juan took just over an hour. Slim's sudden appearance had put Strang in high spirits, and the latter was in an ebullient mood for most of the way. He insisted on asking countless questions about the Danson detective agency and the way it was run, and the problems connected with Strang's own life were pushed into the background.

On the way into San Juan, passers-by began to take notice of Strang and his riding companion. The small community had begun in two distinct sections. One was predominantly Mexican and responsible for many adobe houses. The other was white American and slightly the larger of the two. Board buildings hemmed in a small, squat church around the communal square. Most of the shops and places of entertainment were in the streets a little further away from the centre.

Strang turned into a thoroughfare which had the name, Second Avenue, written up on a board in both American and Spanish. Fifty yards along it, he pointed to the office of the town marshal. The name on the door was Richard Grain, and some writing in smaller letters intimated that the marshal had once been a captain in the U.S. cavalry.

'Wait here a little, amigo,' Strang suggested. 'Grain ain't the sort of man you'd seek out to pass the time of day with. Too thoughtful, too withdrawn. What I have to say will maybe heighten his blood pressure a little.'

Strang swung to the ground and tossed his reins across to Slim, who got down to the ground in more leisurely fashion and took time out to slacken his saddle. Strang walked across the boards to the door and flung it open without ceremony.

'Good day to you, Grain,' he called out, so that his voice carried to anyone close on the street.

'Mr Strang?' The answering voice was one of a lower timbre. Cultured and quiet. 'Something I can do for you?'

'I wish there was, Grain! I surely do. Jest a short while ago I was followed out of town by two cheap rowdies who've been livin' it up in town, probably on stolen money. If I hadn't been alert they'd have had every last cent I had in my pocket, an' maybe shot me into the bargain. They came for me with guns, Marshal, an' that ain't the sort of happening a man of substance ought to have to put up with in these parts! Did you know the men in question were up to no good?'

The quieter voice was raised in protest. The office door was closed from within, and an irate man pushed his face close to the window, as though to ascertain whether they were overheard or not. Slim, who was expecting such a move, took a good look at the countenance of the local peace officer.

The marshal looked to be in his

middle forties. A tall man and a lean one with a pockmarked face and deeply eroded, rather smouldering eyes. His expression was habitually a bitter one, and now, as he felt outraged at the tone of Strang's voice, his nostrils were flaring and the eyes radiating hostility. A stetson with a pointed frontal brim was pushed down hard on the forehead. A black vest flapped, and the figure rocked as he moved away, as though he walked with a limp.

Strang came close to shouting. 'Well, if you didn't take any particular note of the jaspers, at least take a look through your reward dodgers in case they turn up again! You could do yourself an' this community a whole lot of good, if you keep lookin' an' act fast on occasion. Maybe if I give you a full description it would help!'

There was an ominous silence after this outburst, followed by more talk from Strang in a subdued voice. Slim waited patiently, noting the interest which passers-by showed to the impatient stallion which had been given into his care. Obviously, Strang's comings and goings were keenly observed, even if his presence did not radiate warmth in the breasts of his neighbours.

Abruptly, the ex-rancher came out into the open, an unlighted cigar cocked at an angle in his mouth, and a saucy grin spreading over his moustached face. He was chuckling as he remounted and nodding towards the office, where Marshal Grain, and his Mexican deputy, Carlos Garcia, remained cautiously out of sight.

'That gave them something to think about, Slim. Every now and again the local boys have to be given a kick in the pants. Otherwise, in this climate, they go stale and fail to do a useful job.'

'I reckon you don't care much about whether folks like you or not, Mr Strang,' Slim observed, as they left the hitch rail and made their way, side by side, towards the residential area in another direction.

Both of them were smoking cigars when Strang indicated that they had arrived at his house. It was an elegant board house, liberally finished with white paint and green shutters. There was evidence of expensive curtains at the four windows visible at the two-storeyed front, and the small, neat, cultivated garden, suggested careful living, if not exactly good taste.

A mature negro servant with close-cropped snowy hair came around the building as the horses approached the house.

Strang called a greeting to him. 'Howdy, Amos, here I am, back in one piece. I reckon you could be disappointed at that! Here, catch this!'

Strang produced the Derringer pistol from the fold behind his cravat and tossed it to the servant without warning. Amos caught it, and sniffed it. By his expression, he looked to be a perpetual worrier. Now, having sniffed the small weapon and noted that it was empty, he had something on which to focus his anxieties.

'Is you sure you is all right, Mr Strang, sir?'

'Right as rain, Amos, so don't you go worryin' yourself none. Take the horses in back, and then go over that little gun. Maybe it saved my life today, and sure as hell I'll need it again another day. This here is my friend, Slim Blake. Get used to the look of him because he might be around for a few days.'

Slim and Amos exchanged brief greetings while the animals were turned over to the latter. Strang led the way up the steps onto the front porch, and from there into the house, where he suggested that Slim should make himself at home.

Slim's first act on entering was to visit the bathroom and freshen up a little. Ten minutes later, he emerged again and found Strang on the gallery at the back of the house, sitting in a wicker chair. The atmosphere was cooler on that side, and Slim was glad to sink down into a chair which was like the one already occupied.

Newspapers from many counties and two or three territories were scattered about the boards, giving ample evidence of the host's interest in the printed word.

'You feel like talkin' business now, young fellow?'

'If you want the truth, I'm bursting with curiosity, Mr Strang,' Slim admitted, as he crossed his legs and reached for the nearest newspaper.

'That's a good way to be, son, but call me Jason from here on in. Otherwise it ain't goin' to be easy to talk the intimate things which have to be said. I'll jest slip indoors an' fetch one or two pieces of writing which have a bearin' on the case.'

Strang returned in five minutes with some letters which he held in his lap. 'You'll not take it amiss if I avert my face from time to time, Slim, because some of the things I'm goin' to tell you are embarrassin' to say the least. Especially to me, a confirmed bachelor.

'I'll start at the beginnin', if that's possible. Me, I travel around a lot, as you must have guessed. A few weeks ago, my travels took me to Pueblo, in the state of Colorado, north of here. I was there as a sort of rovin' reporter to cover certain celebrations connected with the town's origins some thirty years ago.

'I ain't a one for a lot of hard drinkin' or cavortin' about, but it wasn't possible for me to dodge the convivial atmosphere altogether. Now, one day when I hadn't been there long, I chanced to meet a young woman, Edith Lamont, in a restaurant, and quite by accident. It happened on account of the place bein' crowded and a little on the steamy side. She'd placed herself at my table, the only one in the buildin' which wasn't engaged. I arrived shortly afterwards an' it seemed I was honour bound to offer her the seat. Like a fool, because I was interested in the way she talked, I took up both bills and paid for the eats for both of us.'

'What was she like, this Edith Lamont?' Slim queried quietly, as Strang appeared to dry up.

The moustached man stared at him, coming out of a short reverie. 'I can show you a likeness of her, if you like.'

Slim nodded and leaned forward, keenly interested in this young woman whom he took to be the female villain of the story. Somewhat reluctantly, Strang rendered up the pasteboard likeness of the woman in question. Edith Lamont was a shapely, attractive young woman in her late twenties.

The photograph did not show it, but her hair was the colour of copper, and most times she had it pinned up on the top of her head, a style which made her look even taller than she really was. The frank quizzical eyes which peered out of the photograph were green, in real life. The nose was tilted at the tip. The cheeks were dimpled in a smile, an expression which thinned out the full Cupid's-bow lips.

Slim thought that she could be a real

stunner, if she really tried. He looked up and found Strang studying him shrewdly from under his drawn-down brows.

'She has the shape and carriage of a duchess, if she wants to appear that way,' Strang volunteered, without any special show of emotion.

'Did you go as far as to tell her so, Jason?'

Strang shrugged before answering, as though weighing the question.

'I saw her again, quite by accident, the day after the incident in the café. I was visitin' a barn where a dance was in progress. As I couldn't remain a mere observer all the time without appearin' to be showin' disfavour in the place, I took a couple of whirls round the floor with the others. On the first occasion, this Miss Edith Lamont appeared and hung onto me for most of the dance. The second occasion it happened again, although the men and the women were changing partners. I had to slip a young dude a dollar to take her off my hands.

'She claims we met at a later hour, when no one else was around, but I don't remember that. You'll want to question me, I suppose. All I can say is that I might have gone for a buggy ride at a late hour, but I can't remember.'

Slim's blue eyes flashed with interest. 'How come you are not sure? Did you have a lapse of memory, or were you drugged?'

Strang, who looked very troubled, lost some of the haggardness of his expression as Slim probed after the truth. 'I'll get us a drink before we talk any more,' the host offered.

He left the room and came back with a tray. On it was a jug with a cool liquid in it. There were glasses, and also a bottle of whisky and a separate jug of beer.

'Unlike most men in these parts, Slim, I don't drink strong liquor. My drink is sarsaparilla. Nothing more, nothing less. I find the taste pleasing, and it quenches my thirst. You take exactly what you fancy, eh?'

Slim nodded, thanked him, and helped himself to a glass of whisky.

He said: 'You drank sarsaparilla in Pueblo, and somebody might have doctored it?'

Strang nodded very decidedly. 'There, I think, you've unearthed the truth. Is — is it possible for a man to go on actin' coherently, to move about without staggerin' an' still remember nothing about it afterwards?'

'I think it might be,' Slim replied, frowning with concentration. 'It all depends what was slipped into the drink. Maybe you did stagger, but the young lady didn't want to comment on it. You haven't said, but I think you must have been confined to your hotel room for a time after that day of celebrations.'

'You've guessed right. I gave the owner orders to keep people out. He brought in my meals himself. I could tell by the way he acted that many people were interested in what had gone on the day before. I was frankly puzzled. He made one or two allusions to Miss Lamont, who was by way of bein' a prime favourite in the town — at least with the men.

'You see, in addition to managin' a ladies' outfitters, she did the accounts for a mercantile and a saddler. On top of that, she had the talent to sing in public. She could appear in one or other of the saloons and sing a song without bein' branded as an undesirable. So, when I kept cuttin' the hotelier short about her, he was sort of upset. I began to think things out, and to wonder if something of my old trouble wasn't creepin' up on me. I mean, somebody tryin' to get close to separate me from my fortune.

'Havin' come to that conclusion, I greased a few palms, and as a result I was able to slip away from Pueblo without creatin' any fuss, and without havin' to say goodbye to anyone in particular. Is this all clear so far?'

'Adequately,' Slim assured him, with a brief flash of his crooked smile.

'Maybe we ought to get around to the content of those letters now. It's obvious to me that you've heard from this woman since you came back here.'

Strang nodded, shrugged, and finger-combed his well groomed dark hair across his head. He said reluctantly: 'Well, all right, but go easy from here on in, because I'm awful sensitive about the contents of these letters. I might have burned them before this, only I couldn't show anybody what the woman had in mind, if I did. Here's the first one to arrive.'

Strang handed it over, and Slim took it. The young detective made an effort to keep his face straight as he started to read. Opposite him, Strang began to put up a smoke screen with his cigar.

Creek Villa, Pueblo.

Dearest Jason,

I was so sorry to have missed you the day you left Pueblo for home. Especially after we had been so close the day before.

Believe me, I have met many men in my travels, but I have never encountered a personality as warm as yours, or anyone so generous. This old town will never be the same, now that you have left. The rest of the festivities fell a little flat for me. In fact, our meeting seemed almost like a dream come true. Taking a meal together, dancing at the barn, and then that moonlit buggy ride really enthralled me.

I do so want to believe you asked me to marry you, so if you'll ask me again in your next letter, I'll give the matter serious consideration and you'll almost certainly get your wish!

Yours affectionately,

Edith. XXX

P.S. I can't wait to see San Juan, and your home, dearest.

Having read the letter, Slim gave a faint whistle. He looked up and discovered that his client was staring out across the rooftops and looking far from comfortable. Strang had a poker face behind the big moustache and his true thoughts were hard to ascertain.

'Let me ask you one thing, Jason,' Slim suggested, leaning forward. 'If this little set-up didn't smack of an attempt to get at your money, would you in other circumstances have found Edith Lamont attractive? What I'm sayin' is: are you quite certain that you are a confirmed bachelor?'

The older man's face suffused with colour. 'That's a hell of a question to ask, Slim! If you go on in that vein, I'll begin to wonder who you are workin' for! Take it from me, I wouldn't succumb to this young female's charms if she was the last eligible woman in the West!'

Strang spoke with great fire and fervour, but across from him Slim was not at all sure that the angry talk didn't constitute a smoke screen of a different sort to mask a lot of true emotion. Slim was glad when his host stood up and suggested that they should adjourn to an eating house.

They took the inflamatory letters with them.

5

They took their meal behind a curtain in an alcove at the rear of one of the town's best eating houses. As soon as their stomachs were filled, Strang produced a second letter and handed it across the table. He massaged his well-filled stomach while Slim read it.

The younger man's bleached brows rose slowly up his forehead as he took in the text.

My Own Darling,
  Thank you for your most loving letter, and the answer to your question is 'yes'. I *will* marry you. I love you with all my heart, although we were not together for long. The time has dragged since you went.
  The end of the month seems an age away. Perhaps if I pack my things and come to join you in San Juan a

week early my patience will hold out! Believe me, I am desperate to be Mrs Jason Strang.

Write to me often before the time for me to come, darling, and tell me what you do to pass your time away while we are apart. Until I hear from you, my dearest one.

Your own true love,
Edith. XXXXXX

Slim waved the all-important letter in Strang's direction.

'This — this love letter seems to suggest that you answered the other one in rather warm terms, Jason. This is an answer to a proposal of marriage, apparently written down in a letter. If you really don't want to have anything to do with Miss Lamont, then this letter is a very significant one from the point of view of the law. A truly determined young woman could have a copy of this, jest in case you destroyed it and denied all knowledge of it. If you didn't answer the first letter in the sort of terms she's suggestin', perhaps you have a copy of the letter you sent her?'

Strang's smile was a troubled, weak one. 'I keep copies, in longhand, of all the articles I write for the Press. But I never kept a copy of my letter to this woman. I suppose I neglected to do so because I wanted to forget all about a matter which was troublin' me a lot. You know now why I sent to Amarillo for an able detective. If you like, I could give the gist of what I said in my reply.'

Slim nodded, and eagerly awaited the explanation.

'I called her quite simply 'Miss Lamont', and pointed out that she was labouring under a misapprehension. I admitted to dining with her, but I pointed out that the meeting was quite accidental. The same applied to our meeting at the dance.

'I told her that I had no recollections of a moonlit buggy ride, and that I was a confirmed bachelor with no earthly intention of asking any young woman to marry me. I suggested that if she needed a husband, she should look elsewhere. And so on and so on. Finally, I insisted that she gave over writing to me as her outpourings were distasteful. And this second letter was the reply to that. So, if you didn't think this business constituted a threat earlier on, perhaps now you are convinced.'

Slim nodded. He listened for a moment to muted sounds coming from beyond the alcove. Having satisfied himself that they were not overheard, he leaned forward in a conspiratorial fashion.

'You're under fire all right, Jason. We have to try now and read the mind of the opposition. Is this an all-out effort to get you to part with money to get yourself off the hook before the end of the month, or is this young female determined to come here and force herself upon you? The latter course would call for a lot more effort on her part, but she would have a lot more to gain, if she succeeded.'

Strang was looking his age when he

asked for further explanation of the details.

'I'm no lawyer, Jason,' Slim told him, 'but it seems to me that if you refused to marry her an' she was in a position to produce in court a letter with a proposal in it from you, you might have to part with a substantial sum in the way of damages for a law called breach of promise. Do you see the way this thing could go?'

'All too clearly, amigo,' Strang replied, 'but to get to court she'd have to produce such a letter as you've described. And I've already told you, she ain't never received any letter from me with a proposal in it. So how will she go ahead?'

Slim came out of a brief reverie, during which he had been watching a spider spinning a web on the hickory limb which held their hats.

'Money, in sufficiently large quantities, makes people who want it badly take awful chances at times, Jason. I'm suggestin' that your determined enemy might even consider havin' the letter in question forged. See what I mean?'

Shrewd as he was, Strang had never considered such a contingency. He was so stunned that his cigar fell from his lips and rolled under the table. When he retrieved it, he found Slim on his feet and anxious to take some exercise.

'I've heard a lot today, Jason. Now I need some time to think about it all. I want to be on my own. Give me until, say, tomorrow to come up with a course of action. Believe me, I won't spare myself after that. You'll get value for your money. I'll be along to the house some time before midnight. Don't wait up for me unless you feel like it.'

Slim was more positive now. He did not wait for Strang to approve his course of action. He left without a backward glance.

★ ★ ★

Uppermost in Slim's mind was the possibility that this girl in far-off Pueblo had an ally near at hand. He was contemplating a trip to the town where the girl lived, but before that he felt he ought to try and discover if there was anyone in town who hated Strang sufficiently to bring him down by engineering such a conspiracy as the one which appeared to be developing.

Several casual conversations, and a few greased palms, gave the detective an inkling as to what the town in general thought about writer and ex-rancher Jason Strang. There were few who liked him. Many admired him, but that was a different matter.

Here and there were men who thought they had a grudge against him, but none of them appeared to have the kind of hate which would spark off a campaign which was likely to lead to widespread publicity and a lot of hard feelings revealed in court.

For instance, there was a man who had served briefly with Strang in the same unit in the Civil War. He was drifting around the country, and it was obvious that he had detoured towards San Juan because he hoped to touch his former comrade for a few free meals. The ex-soldier was down in the mouth because many men had already told him that Jason did not take kindly to scroungers and free-loaders.

Another man, one who looked as if he had been in saddles for about forty years, turned out to be a longterm employee of Jason when he was the owner of the Box J cattle ranch. This man had grown impatient of waiting for promotion to segundo or trail boss. He had left of his own accord, and never quite found for himself a job which so well suited him. Now he wanted to go back to the Box J to work for the new owners, the East Coast Cattle Company. Without some sort of reference from Jason, he knew that he stood little chance of being taken on. This character found it hard to ask favours, and he knew from past experience that Strang was slow to deal them out.

These two, and several others, locals,

who wanted to find a way to acquire small amounts of the Strang ample funds, disliked the man because he was better off than they were. But nowhere was there evidence of intense hatred, or the mental ability to set up the threat which was developing through the Lamont girl.

★ ★ ★

Slim turned in late, and slept late the following morning. When he came down to breakfast, he was told by the negro servant that his master had departed for his office. After partaking of a small meal, in the house, Slim was contemplating joining his client at the office.

A breathless runner came up to the house before he left, intimating that Mr Strang would like to see Mr Blake down there right away. Amos trembled a little, unsure of himself as always when his Boss showed signs of being under pressure. Slim did his best to comfort the fellow. He collected his horse and all his equipment, before leaving for the centre of town.

★ ★ ★

A letter from Pueblo had arrived in that morning's mail for Jason Strang. He waved it at Slim across the desk in his sparsely furnished office as soon as the young man stepped indoors.

'Maybe it's later than we think, Slim. What do you make of this?'

The newcomer sank onto an upright chair, which had a slight film of dust on it. He took the letter without comment, and read it.

My Own Darling Jason,

I am writing in haste to tell you that I have almost completed my plans for leaving here and coming to San Juan!

A week has passed by, dearest, and no news from you, but I am not worried — only disappointed. The letter, of course, must have gone astray. My employer, who owns a hat shop, is advertising for a new manageress, while the mercantile store keeper and the saddler, for whom I do accounts, are seeking help elsewhere.

I do hope that I shall be able to assist you greatly in your various interests, when we are together.

Your own devoted and loving
Edith. XXX
XXX

Strang drummed impatiently upon the desk with his nervous fingers. He appeared to be trying to read Slim's thoughts. The young man's expression showed more sympathy than he had revealed before.

'Jason, she surely means business. Up until now I had thought this was a colossal bluff to try and extract some sort of settlement before the time when she could be expected in San Juan. Now, I think, she's prepared to come here and bluff it out. Even if we manage to blow the whole scheme, her presence and insinuations in this town could give you considerable embarrassment. And that means I have to go to Pueblo to try and head her off in some way. Perhaps if I ask around, and show her my professional card, she'll get cold feet. In any case, I have to try. That's what you're payin' your money for. I'll be leavin' inside a couple of hours.'

Strang at once became businesslike, in an effort to be of assistance. He furnished Slim with other letters and documents in his own handwriting which might prove useful for purposes of comparison. The photograph of Edith Lamont also changed hands.

Slim left town without waiting for another meal.

★ ★ ★

The journey to Pueblo, in Canyon County, Colorado, took four days. Covered in trail dust, and slightly the worse for travel, Slim walked the dun into town around four in the afternoon. While the horse was receiving attention in the livery, he booked a room at a hotel and bathed and rested before starting his investigations.

Towards six o'clock, he walked up the sidewalk of the north side of Main Street, and studied the shop windows. At a large mercantile, he bought a few purchases which were everyday necessities, and chatted with the owner who was talkative and exceedingly friendly. The store keeper gave his private views on the best saloons and the shops of people in different lines from his own.

Two doors away, Slim took his first meal since his arrival. He was putting away the second course, a well-cooked apple pie, when a tall, good-looking young woman in a green gown halted outside the street door and casually glanced in through the glass panel. The proprietor, a Scandinavian, waved a hand at her and came out from behind his counter in order to talk to her.

Slim used a mirror on the opposite wall to take a good look at her as she came inside and sat on a stool at the counter to take coffee.

'I'm not hungry enough to eat yet, Swede, but a cup of your coffee will go down well. Sellin' ladies' hats is a dry sort of occupation.'

'Have it on the house, Miss Edie,' Swede suggested, in a tone which suggested that he was happy to have the young woman in the place.

Only two men and a woman were eating in the restaurant besides Slim at the time, but they all looked up and showed polite interest as Miss Edith Lamont parked her elegant frame on the stool and began to slake her thirst.

Slim had recognised her from the photograph, which was a good likeness. She had a warm, pleasant personality, and for the life of him Slim could not imagine her being the central figure in a plot against his client. Her friendly gaze took in everyone, locals and strangers alike. She acted as if she had been in the place many times, and was completely at ease.

'You goin' to take a stroll, Miss Edie, to work up an appetite?' Swede queried, as he dried a pile of clean pots.

'I don't think so, Swede. More likely I'll get along to the Silver Dollar for a while. Andy will be there, and he's good to me. He likes to buy me a drink, as a sort of bonus, over and above what he pays me for doin' the books.'

Edith Lamont was frank in her talk. This was self-evident. She did not mind anyone using the restaurant thinking she was decorative, either. Her hair was as radiant as the photograph had hinted. It was combed and piled high on her crown, with a small green hat resting upon it. A narrow leather belt pulled in her dress at the waist and helped to show shapely ankles beneath the skirt hem. The eyes, green as emeralds, were provocative in the nicest sort of way.

Slim wondered whether he should have approached her then and there.

Normally, he was slower to make contact with people he had to investigate, but this young woman was uncommonly attractive. Almost attractive enough to make him break his own unwritten rules.

At length, she left, with a promise that she would return at a later hour for food. Slim allowed his obvious admiration to show when Swede came to collect his dirty dishes.

'Miss Edie, sir, is jest about the best lookin' unattached young woman in town. I'd say she didn't have an enemy anywhere. And that ain't all. Apart from her good looks, she's more than passin' friendly. I reckon almost anyone in town would do her a favour, if she asked it.'

'I'd like to get to know her better,' Slim remarked fervently.

'Try the Silver Dollar saloon, young fellow, but you'll have to share her with a lot of other admirers down there. Maybe this establishment might be a better spot for a meetin' later on, but

I'd rather you didn't say I said so, if you do meet her here.'

Slim paid his bill and left.

He walked around for over half an hour to settle his food, and then headed for the Silver Dollar, which was already drawing much of its evening custom, due to the sounds of singing and dancing coming from its interior. It was large and spacious, but most of the space was filled by the middle of the evening. Upwards of twenty tables were occupied by men who had been playing card games of one sort and another.

Other tables, slightly further towards the walls than the card tables, held groups of people who had only come to drink. Mostly regular townsmen, with one or two wives in tow.

The four dancing girls had withdrawn from the squat stage by the time Slim managed to get beyond the batwings. He forced his way towards the long bar on the right, using his weight and a little charm where it was necessary.

A bald pianist played a couple of catchy tunes which had a lot of heads turning and tongues wagging. From a door beyond the end of the bar a well-known figure emerged and glanced around him indulgently. Men called to him from the bar. He grinned broadly, acknowledging them all. This was Bill Sando, the proprietor, who was famous in the district, being a former weight-lifter and wrestler. His picture in a wrestling outfit hung over the bar.

He was forty-two now, and a certain amount of fat had formed around his splendid chest and shoulder muscles. His dark quiff was brushed well forward to cover a balding forehead. The short bristling moustache he wore looked exactly the same as the one in the photograph.

Sando cleared his throat, and called out in a voice reminiscent of a prize-ring master of ceremonies. 'Ladies an' gentlemen, it's good to have you with us again tonight. I'm goin' to ask a favour of one of your favourites and mine.' He gestured towards a table set against a wall behind the piano. 'Miss Edith Lamont!'

A great clamour of applause welled up from the closely-packed revellers. In the midst of it, Edith Lamont rose to her feet, smiling happily and still rather glamorous. Beside her, Andy Saddler, a man named like his trade, fanned himself with his derby and beamed, enjoying a certain amount of reflected glory because the young woman had been in his company when called upon to entertain. At fifty, he was pot-bellied and had lost most of his hair.

'Thank you, everyone. Thank you, dear Bill Sando. I will sing for you, if that was what you were goin' to ask. So if you'll jest give me room to get through to the piano, I'll try and think of a suitable piece.'

The uproar, which had died down when the young woman stood up to speak, was now redoubled. Men pushed and heaved to make way for her. Soon, she was seated at the piano, having taken the place of the regular musician. She tinkled a tune out of the ivories, and remained slumped over the keyboard in thought for a while.

When she straightened up, she was ready. The hat was no longer on her head now, and a slight wisp of hair hung becomingly across her forehead. She started to sing in a rather deep voice with a warm, fetching timbre. Her song was sweetly sentimental. It told of a young man who left his sweetheart and crossed the border to make his fortune.

The war came along and made the separation a long one. All through the fighting he had no chance to get back to her. He finished his stint of fighting with a wound or two which had weakened him, and attempted to cross a stretch of formidable desert, so as to reach her side the quicker. A storm made things worse, his horse had to be shot, and the desert claimed him when he did not have far to go. In the last verse, she intimated that it was a mercy he had not made it, because his true love had gone off and married a man fighting on the other side.

The applause was tremendous, but the singer declined to do an encore, and Slim was as disappointed as anyone else in the saloon. He had a couple of whiskies to slake his own thirst, and when he saw the young woman making her excuses to leave, he preceded her.

★ ★ ★

Slim walked the boards long enough to smoke a cigarette. He then returned to the eating house which he had fre-quented earlier. To his surprise, there was no sign of the young woman he sought. The proprietor had retired for a while, and left a Mexican girl to take charge.

Feeling certain that Miss Lamont would go there, sooner or later, Slim went inside and asked for coffee. While he was brooding over it, the Mexican girl approached a door in an alcove, screened by a curtain.

She said: 'If you want anything else, Miss Edie, you jest holler out for me, you hear?'

The sought-after young woman answered as was expected, and Slim rose to his feet and determinedly made his way to the private room. The Mexican girl looked rather shaken at his boldness, but he paused long enough to whisper in her ear that her Boss had suggested this was a good way to meet the young lady.

Shrugging elegantly in an off-the-shoulder peasant blouse, the girl dismissed the matter from mind. Slim knocked and went in. Edith Lamont had a couple of account books on the table where she had been eating her food. Without looking up, she said: 'Okay, Bill, you can take 'em now. There was an error of one hundred dollars in the right-hand column of this one, but I'd say your barmen were honest, even if they are a bit sloppy at times.'

Slim cleared his throat. He waited by the door, toying with his hat. Edith Lamont looked up and was startled.

'Why, young man, who are you? I was expecting Bill Sando from the Silver Dollar! How on earth did you get in here?'

'I saw you here earlier in the evening, and then again at the Silver Dollar a short while ago. As I came a long way specially to see you, as soon as I heard you were in here I came along to present myself.'

The young woman was regarding him in a rather guarded fashion. She had taken a rather elegant pair of spectacles off her nose and put them aside. She seemed to be weighing him up all over again, having recognised him from the earlier occasion.

'May I ask where you have come from?'

'I started out from San Juan, in New Mexico territory. A place where you have special interests.'

Slim was smiling, but he noted that

the news he had just given caused mixed emotions to flash across the woman's mobile features. In a matter of a few seconds, she had her thoughts and her expression under control.

'You must have come from my fiancé, Jason Strang. He isn't hurt or anything, is he? If he is, tell me now.'

'He's sound in wind and limb, Miss Lamont. But he is keen that I should talk to you.'

He sat down, as the woman gestured for him to do so.

6

The Mexican girl must have said something about Miss Lamont's unexpected visitor, because the Scandinavian proprietor appeared and provided them both with fresh coffee. He was there to ascertain whether Slim was a 'wanted' guest or not, and Miss Lamont acted friendly enough for the fellow not to worry about the association.

Slim was slow to come to the point. He lit a cigarette and contemplated the young woman before stating his reason for being in Pueblo.

'Is it something to do with the time of the wedding? *What* is it? Can't you say what you came for? You ought to know that matters like this are very close to a woman's heart.'

Slim turned his head, so as not to blow smoke in her face. He began: 'Miss Lamont, my client, Mr Strang, wants to remain a bachelor. He is most surprised that you should think otherwise. That you should, in fact, think that you are the object of his affection. I ought to tell you at the outset, I know about your letters to him. He thought it best for me to read them.'

The girl clapped an elegant hand over her mouth when the shock hit her. The conflicting emotions showed in her eyes. She was fighting for control, but obviously quite stunned for the moment. He guessed about one question which would be uppermost in her mind.

'I'm an enquiry agent, if you're wondering who I am.'

'Does Jason deny that he ever knew me?' she asked in a voice which sounded as though her throat was restricted.

'No, he met you all right. What he denies is makin' any sort of advances to you, an' he *does* deny writing you a letter which amounted to a proposal of marriage!'

'But that — that's monstrous! And his denial is impossible! Why, I have his letter right here, Mr — whatever your name is! Whatever can he hope to gain by toying with a girl's affections in this diabolical way?'

'My name is Blake. Slim Blake. Jason Strang claims never to have trifled with your affections. He thinks the situation is the other way round. That you are trying to trap him into marriage, in order to get your hands on his money. But you are in a position to verify his advances, if you have his letter, and it is couched in the terms which one of your subsequent letters seemed to suggest. How do you feel about showing it to me?'

'Would it make any difference to your opinion of me, if I showed you his letter?'

'It might do, at that. You must see that letter is of great importance, Miss Lamont. I'd like your permission to examine it rather closely.'

'In what way, rather closely?'

'I'm no expert, but I want to be sure

that it is genuine. I promise you that if you let me have it, no harm will come to it. I will return it to you in the morning.'

Slim privately thought that the girl would have to be naïve to part with the letter to a man in his situation. And then he had second thoughts. If she knew it to be forged, then she would be showing great courage in surrendering it into the hands of a man working for the opposition. He, Slim, knew that he could not destroy the letter if it was genuine, but she was not to know that he had such scruples.

After a time lag of perhaps two minutes, Edith Lamont turned aside and cautiously withdrew the letter in question from the bosom of her dress. It was slightly crumpled in its envelope and smelled faintly of perfume. Slim's nostrils twitched as he took it. Just prior to receiving it he had been smelling the smoke of a strong cigar coming from the direction of the door, which was ajar.

By the light of the lamp over the

table, he opened the letter out, and saw by the first few words under the introduction that it was not the wording which Jason had suggested he wrote.

'I'll be goin' to my room at the hotel, Miss Lamont. There's no fear of my leavin' town with this letter, which, after all, is your property. Rest assured it will be returned. I intend to find out the truth, even if it goes against my client.'

The young woman half-rose to her feet and then subsided again in her chair, nodding for him to go ahead and leave her. Outside the door of the private room, Big Bill Sando came to his feet and blew smoke in Slim's face.

'Eavesdroppin' ain't an occupation I indulge in all that often, young fellow, but I'd jest like to say that nothing had better happen to that letter, if you want to get back to the place you came from in one piece.'

Slim stepped back half a pace from the imposing chest which barred his way. 'I get the meaning of your words, Mr Sando. Here's hopin' neither of us have any sort of explainin' to do in the matter.'

He stepped around the huge ex-wrestler and was allowed to go on his way without further discussion. Sando stepped into the private room to collect his account books.

★ ★ ★

In the privacy of his hotel room, Slim drew down the hanging lamp and perused the letter most carefully. Its actual content intrigued him. If it was a forgery, then it was a most skilful one, composed by someone who could handle words, and, moreover, one who could handle the sort of words which Jason Strang might very well use.

It read as follows:

Jason House, San Juan.
Beloved,
    Your welcome letter has filled me with renewed excitement. I experienced new and deep feelings when

we met, and it was only my doubts about whether I was good enough for you that made me leave without a proper farewell.

I know now that I really did ask you to marry me, and that you did me the honour of giving the proposal serious consideration. By all means, pack up in Pueblo and travel here in good time for the end of the month.

I hope that your decision to become my wife will be one that you will never regret, and I assure you that the days seem long to me, too, in your absence. I pass my time dealing with my affairs and writing articles, but the details would bore you, dear, so enough of this, and I must write again in a few days when I have made the special arrangements for our nuptials.

In the meantime, take care of yourself and take plenty of beauty sleep.

Your intended,
Jason. X

There was nothing special, or significant, about the sort of paper used for
the letter. Under the lamp, the writing
compared very favourably with other
writings definitely penned by Jason on
letters and other things brought along
by Slim. Even the magnifying glass did
not take the baffled look from the
young detective's face.

The magnified work on the vital
letter showed that in places the writer
had taken off the pen, and then gone
over previous letters. But on examination, Strang's own letters revealed that
he had this habit in his own writings.

After pacing the room for upwards of
half an hour in his bare feet, Slim went
to bed with an open mind on the
subject of Edith Lamont and possible
forgery. One interesting thought kept
nagging him. Forgery or no forgery,
Edith was a very interesting woman to
have around. If he ever contemplated
company of a female nature, Jason
could have done a whole lot worse for
himself.

Mindful of his need to make extensive enquiries, Slim was up early and prowling the streets after the lightest of breakfasts. He asked questions about known forgers, men with names like Penman Pete, and Dick Richards. Sometimes he gave their known description, and casually asked if such men had been friendly with Miss Lamont.

Within an hour, his possible informers suffered a change of heart towards him. Bill Sando, or someone else with Edith Lamont's best interests at heart, had put the word around that the young stranger was investigating Miss Edith and working against her best interests.

By the time Slim tackled his first lawyer, his reception was positively frigid. Out on the street again, he began to see the enormity of the task which Strang had given him. The township of Pueblo was wholeheartedly in favour of

Edith Lamont, and, therefore, very much against him and his client. He would get no help from anyone in that area.

* ★ ★ ★

The message was waiting for him on the reception desk when he returned to his hotel to collect the all-important letter at a little after ten in the morning. It was sealed in an envelope: brief and to the point. It indicated that a friend of Jason Strang would like to talk to Slim Blake at the Studebaker shack, west of town, as soon as possible. Slim glanced up at the staircase, and thought about the letter.

His interest in this possible contact made him leave the letter where it was. Instead, he turned on his heel and went outside again, hurrying to the livery to collect his horse. He had a feeling the Studebaker cabin might be a mile or two beyond the town boundary.

In this supposition he was right.

7

As soon as he saw the rather derelict looking cabin nestling in a hollow on a grassy slope he started to feel easier. Many a man looking for information had been lured into the open and attacked, in his experience. But this cabin was a little too exposed. If Studebaker wanted to know about the approach of his fellow humans in the days when it was occupied, he had picked a good spot.

Nevertheless, Slim used a lot of caution. He dismounted and shooed the dun down the slope to where distant thick foliage suggested the possibility of water. The animal went willingly enough, and was soon lost to view, cropping the grass as it wandered along, utterly unconcerned with the immediate future.

The horse's attitude helped to put its

master a little more at ease. He tiptoed into the dusty dwelling with his .45 in his hand, but no one attempted to jump him. The only sign of recent occupation was a tiny piece of paper pinned down on a rocky table by a chipped coffee mug. A faint breeze from a broken window was stirring the paper.

No one suddenly appeared from the loft or darted in behind him, as he crossed to the table and picked up the message. It was a simple one.

Come down to the creek. This is a little too obvious.

More intrigued than ever, he took the advice, walking easily down the slope which was well grassed and stunted with shrubs between scrub oak and pines which blocked the view. Fifty yards below the shack, he got his first glimpse of water. The creek had movement in it, and the faint ripples along the bank, which was liberally screened with willows, made a soothing sound which drew him on.

Excitement beaded Slim's brow and

upper lip with perspiration. He removed the bright red bandanna from his neck and dabbed himself with it. The revolver was back in its holster now. Having tackled his face and brow, he hauled off his well-worn stetson and wiped the inside band. The tousled fair hair with the sandy tints in it was mussed up before it was covered again.

He wondered who in the Pueblo area would prove to be a friend to Jason Strang. Or did the summons really mean that Edith Lamont had an enemy? He felt sure that he was in for some sort of revelation within a mere few minutes. The water drew him. The terrain levelled out as he approached it, heading for the line of willows.

His alert mind told him that if he was still likely to be attacked it would be while he was quenching his thirst. He remembered tales about jungle water-holes, and how predators waited near them to attack weaker animals. He licked his lips, which were dry, slowed his pace, and gradually looked over the ground he had traversed from all angles. No one was following him. No restless bushwhacker's horse gave away its master's presence.

A taller tree than the willows, standing high at the near bank, drew him towards it. Still no sign of the friend of Jason Strang. Swaying foliage above his head gave him an idea. He divested himself of the swinging leather vest and jumped upwards to catch hold of a tree branch which grew at a convenient height. A deep breath and a quick heave put him in a position to draw himself up onto the limb, where he was able to crawl out along it. From that vantage point, he studied the far bank. There were birds and one or two small animals in evidence, but no men.

To ease his position, he stretched out along the limb and again peered around him. He was shaping up to yawn when the first of the hostile bullets whined towards him from tree cover some fifty yards or so behind him on the same side of the creek. Within seconds, a minor fusillade of revolver fire intimated that he had, in fact, run into trouble and that his attackers did not much care if their bullets hit him.

His nerves were jumping as the small missiles ripped through the branches and leaves about him. He pushed out his right hand, reached for a lesser branch growing out of the one which held his body, and experienced a sharper shock. No sooner had he grasped the lesser limb than a bullet severed it inches from his hand.

As his weight was partially resting on it, he lost his balance and pitched towards the bank without warning. A little of the cat's agility in him made it possible to avoid hitting the earth with his head. He rolled on his shoulders, but failed to stop his general slipping towards the water.

He blinked several times and grounded his elbows, mindful of the fact that his old cuts and bruises had only just mended in time for the long trip into this area. With other meetings likely between himself and Edith Lamont, he wanted no more cuts and contusions which needed explaining away.

More bullets kicked into the grass of the bank. He slowed his momentum under the hanging screen of willow, but not in sufficient time to stop himself from sliding down the steep bank and into the water. He went head first and quite gracefully, very like a seal entering water.

Surface water lifted his hat, making it bounce an inch or two and sending it out into the current, where it floated towards his right. Slim was no stranger to swimming in water. His mind worked swiftly as the cool waters closed over his head. His attackers would come at least to the edge of the bank and take more potshots at him. That much was obvious. He had never seen nor swum in this particular stream. What should he do?

His revolver sailed out of the holster and overtook his head, trailing bubbles on its way to the stream bed. Blinking hard, and holding his breath, he propelled himself towards a brighter patch of water where powerful sun rays shone to the bottom through a gap in the trees.

There, he took a brief glimpse of what lay below him. Acting upon impulse, he turned about adroitly in the water and swam back towards the bank. Long, groping tree roots came out to meet him and pulled him up short. The air in his lungs wanted changing, so he drifted upwards, struck his mouth cautiously above the surface and breathed out and in.

He stayed there with his chest working hard. Occasionally he turned his head and listened. What he heard left him in no doubt that men, probably three in number, were down at the water's edge having a good look around for him. One man with a certain sense of humour was blasting away at the drifting hat and hitting it more times than he missed it. Others were firing their guns haphazardly, as though trying to hit him under the water, although they could not see him.

When their guns were empty, they desisted. The atmosphere quietened considerably. Slim's breathing had eased, but his heart thumped uncomfortably when he reflected that they had only to look sharply down at their feet to see his outline against the roots at the foot of the bank.

Five minutes dragged by like five hours. After that, the gunmen appeared to be satisfied. Before they withdrew there was a short consultation on the bank.

One said: 'Kind of strange, the way it turned out.'

'Yer, I don't figure any of us thought he'd end up in the stream. Still, that was purely accidental. We could say we frightened him to death!'

This sally brought forth roars of laughter. When it had subsided, the first speaker had another query. 'Do you boys reckon we shot him in the water, or what?'

A fresh voice suggested: 'He could have hit an underwater obstruction and drowned. That would be my guess. But what does it matter? All we have to do is get out of the area and keep quiet about it. If either of you have designs on his hoss, forget about it. That sort of attitude leads to mistakes.'

The boots walked away, clinking spurs, and Slim was left alone. He was very slow to come out of the water, and when he had done so he went back in again almost at once to dive for his missing revolver. That took three dives and a lot of energy, but he managed it, and the weapon had to be dried out and cleaned as soon as he got back to the dun and his saddle pockets.

A ride of two hundred yards down the side of the creek brought him to the place where his much ventilated hat was trapped in an eddy of water under a sagging tree branch. Angered about its treatment, he screwed as much water out of it as he could before hanging it on his saddle horn to dry.

On the way back into town he started thinking all over again. There was no sort of a lead as to who had sent the ambushers to deal with him. All he could do was keep his eyes open for them in the future. Again, this would be difficult because he had never set eyes on them. There was just one possibility which might pay off. Edith Lamont was somewhere mixed up in all these happenings.

He decided to make for the row of wooden terraced houses where she lived known as Creek Villas, and see if anyone entered or came away from there who might have been one of his attackers.

★   ★   ★

The return to the vicinity of Creek Villas took less than half an hour. Slim's horse was still among the tree belt some fifty or so yards from the block of four dwellings when the little man scuttled out of Edith Lamont's front door and darted into the undergrowth on the far side of the dwellings.

Slim was so surprised that he jerked the dun to a stop. He had recognised the furtive figure at the first glance, but he felt sure that he had not been looking at one of the men who had attacked him. Of Edith Lamont herself there was no sign. Nor did anyone appear at the doors or windows of the other dwellings.

Giving off moisture in the form of steam, Slim waited and wondered what to do. He was in no shape to go visiting a young woman, in the event that she was at home. Moreover, he could not imagine her having sent three slap-happy gunmen to frighten him off, either. If they were acting on her behalf, they were under the orders of someone else, for sure.

Shrugging rather disconsolately, he turned the dun about and headed it in the more general direction of the centre of town.

Derby Jones, he was thinking. A small sneak thief, put away on evidence collected by one James Blake, otherwise known as Slim. A small tricky little thief of a man, who had once earned a comparatively honest living as a race-course jockey. Jones was pint-sized; forty-two years of age and permanently dishonest in a small way. When in funds he bought lots of strong liquor which made his bulbous eyes look red about the whites, and slightly sinister.

Derby would certainly go to great lengths to do him, Slim, a disservice, but he was not the type to take a gun to an old adversary. So he didn't need to have any connection with the three ambushers. Nevertheless, it was interesting to know that a man like Derby Jones could enter Edith Lamont's dwelling and leave unnoticed.

It occurred to him that Derby might have been in the act of robbing the Lamont girl, but this possibility was dismissed. Derby was loath to rob known and well-liked women. Besides, he usually worked in the centre of towns, in and around the hotels.

★ ★ ★

Two surprises awaited Slim in the ensuing hours. The first one he learned about within half an hour of reaching his room. The all-important letter which might have been a forgery had been removed from the place where he left it. That was a shaker, indeed. He fought down a strong impulse to go in search of Edith Lamont and try and trick her into admitting that she had received it back into her own care.

Somehow, he managed to fight off the impulse. He stripped off all his damp clothing and changed into dry gear. After sleeping for two hours on the bed, he sauntered out again, determined to take up his investigations where he had left off, even though most of the residents were hostile to him.

This time, he soon became aware that Edith Lamont was harder to find.

Certain knowing townsmen and women were looking at him and smiling. Presently, he found out why. Edith Lamont had packed up and left town by stagecoach. She had travelled towards the south.

* * *

Jason Strang was seated at his favourite table at eight o'clock in the evening in the dining-room of San Juan's principal hotel at the end of that week when Edith Lamont walked in upon him and took him completely by surprise.

He had his back to the door, and so did not see her enter the room. A helpful waiter with wide black side-burns pointed out the Strang table, thinking that he was doing both parties a service, and watched with mounting interest as the personable young woman hastened towards Jason's chair with her bottle-green skirt delicately hitched away from her ankles.

People at the three other occupied

tables were also aware of what was going on. Edith crouched over towards Jason, keeping behind his shoulder and turning towards the other diners with a becoming blush on her rounded fresh-looking cheeks. The expressions on the faces of the others appeared to encourage her in what she was about to do.

A whiff of perfume teased the nostrils of the feeding man. His shoulders stiffened. Edith chuckled, very close to him. Her emerald-green eyes were full of mischief as he turned and looked her full in the face.

'Why, Jason,' she murmured, in a voice which carried, 'I do believe you are overdoin' your surprise. Do you want these good folks to think you don't know me? When our marriage is only a few days away?'

Strang's mouth moved, but he knew not what to say. His knife and fork remained poised above his food. Half-chewed food in his mouth almost choked him. He gave out with a half-strangled noise.

'Jason, are you shy about me comin' along and meetin' you in public? You shouldn't be, darling.'

At last, Strang managed to clear his mouth and his throat. He was visibly very angry. 'Madam, Miss Lamont, I sent you a letter . . . ' he began.

'I know, darling, and I accepted! Please ask me to sit down, Jason!'

As he appeared to be in the grip of emotions which robbed him of his speech, she sat down opposite to him and poured for herself a tumbler of water.

'Darling, when we met back there in Pueblo, I had no idea how unused you were to the company of women. I can see that I'll have to handle you very carefully.'

Strang threw down his eating irons, spilling a small amount of food on the cloth. He turned round and glared at the waiter, but that worthy fellow's attention was deliberately in another direction. Abruptly, Strang rose to his feet, sending back his chair with the backs of his legs.

'Woman, you're up to some dishonest scheme. That I'm sure of! I wrote to you denyin' any interest in you. I sent a man to make it even more clear, and here you are in my home town pestering me again with trumped-up charges about an offer of marriage. If you know what is good for you, you'll leave this town in the very near future, and, until you do leave, keep out of my way. Believe me, I have considerable influence in these parts, and I won't hesitate to use it against you!'

Having said his piece, Strang threw down his table napkin, loosened his cravat with a nervous finger and headed for the door. He snatched his hat off the stand in such a fashion that the whole article almost fell across the floor. Without a backward glance, he left the room and the building.

The waiter glanced at each of the other occupied dining tables and shrugged his shoulders. The new arrival, looking rather lost and weeping silently into a small square of handkerchief, presented a problem. He was half-way towards her, not knowing exactly what to suggest, when a man dining alone at a nearby table intervened.

Buckeye Gorden, a travelling salesman, was fairly well known in San Juan. He was in his late forties, an energetic, portly man with flattened brown hair streaked across his bald, egghead skull, and a large formidable brown glass eye which focused everyone's attention on it.

'Miss Lamont, I believe?' he remarked, rising to his feet. 'I'd be glad to have you join me, if you will. You won't remember me, but I've made your acquaintance in Pueblo on occasion.'

Edith appeared to be too downcast to make the trip to another table, despite the other's friendliness, but Gorden went over to her and took her by the elbow, insisting. When she was seated, he ordered for her, and talked in a loud voice for all to hear who wanted to eavesdrop.

'As a matter of fact, Miss Lamont, I saw you an' Mr Strang keepin' company in Pueblo a few weeks back, at the time of the festivities. I must say that I'm utterly dumbfounded at the reception he gave you, when you obviously came all this way to be with him. He must have taken leave of his senses, and that's for sure.'

In his apparent efforts to soothe the distracted young woman, Gorden made it clear that his sympathies were all with her, and not in the slightest in Strang's favour. The other groups of diners slowly dispersed, but not before they had heard a whole lot more gossip which was fine material for the garbled stories they were about to put around the town.

8

As is often the case with men who have made a lot of money and not offered it around, Jason Strang was one who had many acquaintances but few real friends. In making the Box J the thriving outfit it turned out to be, he had trodden on many corns. And now, this hint that all was not well with the man they had to respect made it easy for people to take in the 'marriage' gossip and think the worst of him.

Speculation about the aloof writer and the startlingly attractive young woman who had come to town swearing she had been sent for to be his bride was on everybody's tongue. Strang's prestige began to be undermined. Fancied slights going back over the years became exaggerated in the minds of people who had been forced to show him respect for longer than they cared to admit.

The talk was that he was tight with his money, and that he trifled with the affections of young women when he went away on long trips supposed to be connected with his writings.

* * *

The ranchers Wayne Malloy and Sam Wardle were just two men who were anxious to think the worst of a man who had proved a better rancher along the South Creek Basin, and one who had outdone them in controlling the rights which ranchers needed to expand their property.

Seated on the select side of San Juan's most frequented saloon, they nursed several fingers of whisky apiece and talked about their common grievances. Malloy was a thin man in his middle forties, with buck teeth and greying hair and beard. Wardle was several years his junior in age, a hefty man with a large family. The boundaries of their land adjoined the ranch which still used the Box J brand.

Malloy was saying: 'One thing I know, it takes a long time to know another man, to really know him, out here in the West. I mind the time when you an' me, and two or three others with interests along South Creek Basin, attended a bit of a shindig at the Box J, early on in Jason's day.

'I guess you'll remember how we burned into the woodwork of his big fireplace our own brand marks, as a sort of insurance against ever going against each other. And yet where did it get us?'

Big Sam Wardle cleared his throat rather noisily. 'I know what you are gettin' at, Wayne. How Jason treated us over those water rights. You wanted the use of water which was not far on his side of the boundary between your two spreads. When he refused you the right to use any part of it, you had to develop in another direction where the grass was not as good and the ground uneven.'

Malloy was nodding as though he would never stop, and all the while applying his whisky glass to his fleshy lips.

'My problem was a different one,' Wardle went on, 'but it shook down to the use of water, once again. All I wanted to do was redirect some of that spring water comin' down from the distant hills, but would he allow my hands to dam it? He would not, to help me, and because of that my outfit has never prospered like it could have done.'

Malloy patted him on the shoulder and refilled his glass from the bottle. 'If I'd have known now what I did then . . . I mean, if I'd known then what I do now, you an' me, we could have raised funds somehow an' bought the Box J when he decided to retire.'

'But he sold it to the East Coast Cattle Company, instead of givin' any local man a chance,' Wardle pointed out. 'Do you think he would have sold out to us, if we'd had the money, because *I* don't! I think he don't like to know people too well, in case they make any calls on him, like friendship, for instance.'

Wardle's voice was beginning to slur under the influence of the potent whisky. His eyes were growing heavy when Wayne Malloy knocked over his glass and caught it again before the liquor spilled.

Wardle, seeing what he had done, shook with laughter. Malloy, who was no more in control of himself than Wardle, joined in, so that they shook and almost wept for nearly five minutes. At the end of that time, Wardle fought to say something, but it was another five minutes before his words made sense.

'All — all that money, him keepin' it to himself, an' now this young female comes along and catches him right where it hurts! In the pocket, Wayne, in the pocket! I hope she gets him good, gets him hogtied before he knows what's happened to him. What do you say, pardner? It's your turn to talk!'

'My — my sentiments exactly, Sam. I hope she spends it faster than he took to make it. I'd sooner make a friend out of a rattlesnake, so help me, that's the gosh-durned truth!'

★ ★ ★

Slim Blake dismounted at the hitch rail in front of the Strang residence around ten o'clock the following morning. He was surprised to find his employer still in the house, though he was fully dressed as though ready to go out to his town office. He was smoking the very short end of a cigar with his diamond stick pin stuck through it to hold it, but he soon discarded that when he set eyes on his travelling aide.

'What in tarnation kept you away this long, and out of touch, Slim? That young virago of a woman is right here in this town, and almost everyone has turned against me because of what she said in a public place!'

The two men met on the gallery, each more angry than the other had anticipated.

'Stop goin' off at half-cock, Jason, an' cool down a bit, otherwise you'll have a heart attack or something. Doggone it, what's the matter? Is the sarsaparilla gripin' your stomach? For a man with your background, you are soon depressed! I guess you are out of cigars, too, and you don't want to go down into town and buy some more. Why don't we go through to the back and exchange ideas? There's a lot to be said, and we might as well say it in private an' be comfortable.'

Jason at once agreed. He was beginning to feel better now that Slim was with him. He had never doubted that the young man would work hard for his money. But the sudden, unheralded arrival of Edith Lamont in town, without any prior warning from Slim, had badly shaken him.

As soon as they were seated, Slim asked who should talk first. Strang had so far recovered his self-possession that he wanted to listen. So Slim expounded, at length. He delivered himself of his doubts and uncertainties, and gradually brought his client up to date.

'It's true I could have warned you by telegraph that she might be comin' this way, but I never knew for sure where she was headed for. Besides, my treatment back in the state to the north had rather shaken me. If you have any doubts, take a look at my hat! Four bullet holes in it, and the same might have happened with my head in it, if the hat hadn't been forced off by the pressure of water when I slid into the creek. I still don't know to this day whether those bushwhackers intended to kill me or not. For my money, they were actin' far too tough, an' not carin' particularly about the outcome.'

Jason sniffed. He crossed to a small wooden cabinet and extracted from it a packet of factory-made cigarettes which he would never have smoked when he had cigars. He patted Slim on the shoulder, and offered him one which he took gratefully.

Casually almost, Strang returned to his seat. 'I'm intrigued to know that you had your hands on that vital letter, the one which had to be a forgery, Slim. And then you had to lose it. Sorry if I sound disappointed, but everything from a legal point of view seems to rest on that piece of writing. And now we don't have it. The point is, what do we do now?'

Slim shrugged. He felt that this was a time when an older man's advice might have been better. Someone such as Horace Danson, his Boss, might have known what to do, although this case had all the earmarks of being unique.

'Well, Jason, we're still a few days away from the end of the month. If you're bein' taken to court for a broken promise, nothing will happen until that time, except, perhaps, one or two rather painful and embarrassing encounters. Me, I'm about to start lookin' all over again at this end. During the last hour of my ride, I got to thinking that I might get a lead out on your old property, the Box J.

'There has to be somebody in these parts who feels very strongly about you, hates you, in fact. I'm lookin' for somebody full of hate, with the brains to set up your sort of trouble.'

'Go to the Box J, by all means, if you think it will help,' Strang approved, 'but I'll be surprised if you find a tie-up in or near this town with our Miss Lamont from Pueblo.'

And Slim did leave, within the half-hour; as soon as his mount was rested and groomed.

★ ★ ★

Almost an hour later, Vincent Rockall came out onto the long worn gallery of the Box J ranch house and studied the approaching rider through powerful telescope lenses. Apart from his stetson, which he brushed carefully every day, Rockall talked, acted and dressed like a Boston accountant from the north-east coast.

He was a neat, dapper individual with a well-groomed silver thatch of hair, black barred brows and a red face. His grey eyes were curiously lacking in expression. He wore a white shirt habitually, and a string tie which was always neatly tied. His dark business suit might have graced any number of professional offices in his native Massachusetts.

Men said of him that he looked more unlike a Western rancher than any other man on earth. But he kept his ordinary hands well under control due to the influence of two twin-gunned segundos whom he had imported from another state at the time when he took over control.

The fair-haired man coming to visit rode the dun horse as though trail riding was his principal interest in life, and yet he did not look like a man coming to ask for work. The blacksmith hobbled over to the gallery, holding his hand to a tired back.

'This here fellow looks uncommonly like the stranger workin' for Jason Strong, Boss. You want that I should stop him at the gate?'

'No, let him come on up here. I'd be interested to know what he has to say.'

And that was the way it was. Within a few minutes, Slim walked his horse across the paddock and tied it to a rail below the gallery. He touched his hat. Rockall signalled for him to come up and talk, and Slim took the second wicker chair on the gallery, having lifted an old saddle out of it to make room for himself.

A half-breed woman appeared from the house, bowed when the Boss nodded, and went indoors again to produce coffee.

'Well, sir, this is the Box J cattle outfit. I'm Vincent Rockall, the manager, as you probably know. You are a stranger to me. What can I do for you?'

'Good day to you, Mr Rockall, I don't want to take up too much of your time. I'm James Blake, known as Slim. Looking into the affairs of Mr Jason Strang. Would you talk to me for a few minutes?'

Rockall frowned, and then smiled, showing widely spaced teeth, all his own. 'Are you thinking that he still has his money sunk in this enterprise? It's almost a year since I came here, and he'd sold out before that. I really don't have much experience of him since then. He's a busy man, so they tell me. A writer.'

Rockall said the word writer as though he meant that Strang was the opposite of busy. Slim noticed this, but he did not comment on it.

'I know he sold out his interests to the East Coast Cattle Company, but I was wondering if you could help me. You see, there's a whole lot of infamous talk goin' on in San Juan about Mr Strang. Wild talk which is being started by a young woman from Colorado. Now, I've talked to the woman in her own home town, and I know there's some mystery around her assertion that Mr Strang wanted to marry her.

'My own view is that there is a conspiracy afoot. An attempt to blacken the character of my client, Mr Strang. Even perhaps to cheat him out of his considerable fortune. Could you tell me of anyone who hates the man sufficiently to be a party to such a conspiracy?'

'Why come to me, Mr Blake? I'm an Easterner with little reason to feel strongly about Jason Strang. If it is of any interest to you, I scarcely ever buy the papers which print his articles. Mine come from the East Coast, mostly Boston and Philadelphia. Unless I'm very much mistaken, you've had this long ride out from town to no avail.'

The coffee arrived while Slim was shrugging his shoulders. He took the proffered cup and tipped a lot of sugar into it before putting it to his lips and slaking his thirst. The woman put milk and sugar into a second cup, stirred it up and left it by the manager's elbow. Then she withdrew.

'Do you have any sort of reactions in regard to Jason Strang from your neighbours, Mr Rockall? Perhaps your company bosses have definite views about him.'

Rockall sipped his coffee. For a minute or so, he seemed to be indifferent about answering. His brows went up when he had thought over the latest questions. 'The Box J is snug behind its own boundaries, Mr Blake. I have very little contact with the other ranchers in the basin. In any case, on the infrequent occasions when we meet, we don't discuss the previous owner. As for my bosses, all I can say of their views is that they consider Strang drives very hard bargains. More than that I really cannot say. Most of the hands have been changed since Strang's time, so you'll forgive me if I ask you to leave as soon as you have finished your coffee.'

Slim took his dismissal with a good grace. He remained quite polite as long as he was on Box J soil. On the way back, he had to confess to himself that he had learned little through his visit. The Box J headquarters had proved to be impressively big, but more than that he had not learned.

It was very unlikely that anyone currently on Box J land had anything to do with the Edith Lamont affair.

★   ★   ★

The ride back into town dragged a little, but as soon as the dun had carried him within the town's boundary, he began to hear the voices again. Half-way along one of the main streets, he passed a lawyer's office. The upper half of the window was open, and a conversation drifted out to him. It was almost as if the voices had been raised for his benefit.

An authoritative voice was saying that

if Edith Lamont had proof that Jason Strang had proposed marriage and been accepted, and that he was now seeking to slide out of his bargain, he could most definitely be taken to court and made to pay for the error of his ways, if the lady should so desire it.

Slim hurried on, whistling quietly to himself, as though the noise gave him company.

9

Anyone could be forgiven for grumbling at two o'clock in the morning. Strang's servant, old Amos, was no exception, but his current worries concerned the imminent departure of his master to a secret hideout.

'Mr. Strang, if you have to leave your house an' go into hidin' in the country, why don't you let me come with you? I ain't all that old that I can't face up to a week or two in a shack, so help me! I was born in one, sir!'

Strang, who was in a bitter mood, turned away from the pack he was strapping on the back of his stallion, and patted the old negro on the shoulder.

'I know how you're feelin', Amos, an' I appreciate it. I don't want to leave, but I think Slim's argument about hidin' out for a short while is a good one. So don't give it any more thought. You can't go with me because somebody has to take charge of the house while I'm away. If you wanted you could go and sleep at the house of your friend down the other end of town. All the place needs is a little dusting and such every now and then, and the curtains openin' in the daytime.'

'Nothing is goin' to happen to Mr Strang, Amos,' Slim added. 'All this activity is simply to save him a lot of embarrassment in the next few days. In any case, I'll be around to give you any help you need an' advise you. So off you go back to bed, and leave things to us. You hear me?'

The servant had come to have a lot of confidence in Slim. He managed an uncertain smile, and a few minutes later retreated indoors to watch the departure from a window. Strang and Slim both waved to him before mounting up and walking their horses away from the residential section.

Strang was chewing on a dry cigar.

139

Every now and then he thought of something to grumble about. 'If you ask me, San Juan and district is dead from the point of view of clues about my troubles. I don't like pullin' out of town like this, either. Hundreds of people will take my action as a sign of guilt. They'll be fully convinced before any courtroom lawyer tries to prove it that I offered Edith Lamont marriage. Still, as you suggest, it might be best to dodge people for a day or two. I wish I hadn't mentioned Bobcat's Retreat, though. That shack sure is a retreat. It's directly on the route to Red Rock Canyon, an' everybody knows that's a no-exit place. That's why folks stay away.'

'All the more reason why you should use it right now, Jason. It's no use thinkin' of hidin' in a spot, where anyone can find you. If you think about it, you'll see that's so.'

Strang did think, and he became silent. An hour later, the two horses started down the remote draw to where

140

a once-wild old prospector addicted to rum had made his lonely abode.

★ ★ ★

A little after half past four in the morning, Slim arrived back at the Strang house, and was fussed over by the anxious servant, as though he had been the master. Before five o'clock Slim was asleep, and the sun had been up for a couple of hours before Amos thought to rouse him with a strong cup of coffee.

The visitor partook of a light breakfast, and sat himself down at the master's desk to make some notes on the details of the case, as he knew them this far. The making of the notes promoted a lot of thought, but no new clues popped up as a result of the mental exercise. The heavy grandfather clock in the lounge-cum-study was whirring, prior to striking twelve for midday, when the knocking came at the front door.

Amos, who had been polishing silver, came into the room where Slim was seated with a duster in his hand.

'It — it's a young lady, all dressed up, arrivin' in a buggy, Mr Slim. What'll I do now?'

Slim's face brightened with interest. 'Why, answer the door, Amos, and if the young lady's business is with the master, show her in to me. I think I know who it will be.'

The young detective grinned to give the servant confidence. He found himself rising to his feet and checking that his morning shave had been a good one in a mirror. He had changed his outfit after the night ride, and felt reasonably presentable to receive a young woman specially done up to make a call.

Amos' mute face was full of enquiry as he held open the door for Edith to enter. She was wearing an outfit which Slim had seen before, but to Amos everything about her was new. Slim came to meet her. He gestured towards

142

a comfortable high-backed armchair, and suggested that Amos should prepare coffee for two.

Edith looked surprised when she found Slim in charge of the house. Her mobile expression showed that she was intrigued with the interior décor, and perhaps a little relieved not to find Strang ensconsed and hostile.

She murmured: 'Why, Mr Blake, this is a long way from Pueblo. My business is very personal, and with the master of the house, as you know. I hadn't thought to see you here.'

She took the chair, however, and made a tiny adjustment to the small green hat which topped her intriguing mound of copper-coloured hair.

'As you say, Miss Lamont, San Juan is a long way from Pueblo. I thought you left Pueblo in rather a hurry. Mr Strang is out on business for a few days, so perhaps this gives me an opportunity to finish off our conversations which started in your home town.'

'Is there no chance that I can talk to

my fiancé today or tomorrow?' Edith asked, frowning slightly.

Slim sat down opposite to her, shaking his head. 'Mr Strang is definitely out of town for a few days. He went on my advice, you see. Your arrival here, and the manner of your meeting with him, has turned the local population against him. In a way, you have defamed his character.'

Tiny spots of colour formed around the young woman's high cheekbones. Her breast rose and fell, also showing signs of deep emotion.

'Slim Blake, you sound more like a lawyer than a detective. Suddenly I want to see the last of you. I don't think I'll wait long enough for coffee.'

She said this as if she meant it, but made no move to get up out of the chair. Instead, she tapped the floor with the ferrule of her decorative umbrella. Slim gave her time to settle down. His mind was busy. He was trying to think up a way of saying what he had to say which might startle her into making revelations about this whole troublesome affair.

He said: 'Miss Lamont, you are a woman of many parts. I wonder if you are the friend of Jason Strang who sent me the message to go to the Studebaker cabin, west of Pueblo?'

He studied her face, saw that she clearly looked stunned by his question. He was distracted a little, reminded what an attractive woman she was, whether she was acting normally, or just acting. He rose to his feet and fetched his stetson, which was now very much the worse for wear.

He was standing in front of her, spinning it on his finger, when she answered.

'Me, no, I didn't send you any message. Why should I? I thought you were an intruder in my life. I hadn't any special wish to see you again.'

He busied himself, poking a little finger through the various bullet holes in the crown of the hat. 'No, but someone was keen to meet me. They lured me out to the shack, then down to the creek, and finally emptied at least three cylinders of bullets at me and my hat. If I hadn't been a useful swimmer I'd be dead now, and all because I was investigatin' *you* for Jason Strang! Now, what do you say to that? How many lethal friends do you have helpin' you in this get-rich-quick scheme?'

'Slim, I'm sorry, but I know nothing about this attack on you, or — or of your insinuations about me and Jason's money. I — I came here to talk about marriage an' love, not — not defamation of character an' the other crimes I'm supposed to have committed, so there!'

Amos' quiet knock at the door seemed out of keeping with the tense atmosphere building up in the room. Slim gestured for the tray to be left on a low table between the two occupied chairs. The old man paused as he retired for an extra look at his master's man and the rather disturbing young lady visitor.

Edith was sipping coffee when Slim opened up again.

'I think you made a tactical error when you left Pueblo without seein' me again, because I hadn't returned your letter to you before you left.'

Edith's cup rattled in the saucer as she grounded it, visibly shaken by this blunt utterance. Slim followed up his advantage.

'That letter could still be a forgery. It could put you in prison, and yet you left for this town without it, knowing that Jason was anything but willing, and that he would have to be pressed into marriage. *I suggest that you didn't wait to receive the letter back because you already had it!*'

The green eyes flashed fire at him. The dimples were back in the cheeks due to the severity of Miss Lamont's expression. She grounded the coffee cup rather heavily.

'Oh, but that is too much! Now you are suggestin' that in some way I stole it back from you! Petty theft to add to my other crimes! Really, Slim, that's too much!'

She rose briskly to her feet, but did not head towards the door. She knew that Slim had further revelations to make, and that she ought to hear them, whatever the consequences of her recent actions.

'I headed straight for your house when I got clear of the creek and the Studebaker place. I was jest in time to see a known sneak thief, Derby Jones, come out of your front door and run away. I'd say Derby was the one who stole the important letter out of my room and returned it to you! How much did you pay him, Edith?'

'I — I never heard of such a thing, or such a man as Derby Jones. Maybe your imagination is too vivid, Slim Blake. You appear to be confused about a lot of things, but I'm not stoppin' here to explain, or to be insulted further. I'll bid you good day!'

And with that, the visitor headed for the door, brushing heavily against the coffee table as she went. Old Amos had to stand aside as she headed for the front door and let herself out without further ado. Half a minute later, Slim and Amos were standing side by side at the front gate, watching the buggy going away in a low cloud of dust.

'I sure am glad you was here to talk with that lady, Mister Slim. She's kind of formidable, ain't she? Mr Strang is mighty good with the men, but I don't know how he might have made out with her. I guess you know best. He *is* better out of town for a while.'

Slim turned and patted the old man on the shoulder. 'Her visit has not done Mr Strang's business any harm, Amos. Don't go broodin' over it. Things could be worse.'

Amos went indoors, and retired to the kitchen, chuckling quietly to himself. After pacing up and down for a few minutes, Slim returned to the lounge. This time he crossed to the desk, and opened one of the lower drawers with a key which Strang had left for him. Two or three account books only merited a cursory glance, but a leather-bound diary was pulled out and opened on the desk top.

Sometimes, the source of a man's troubles were right under his nose, and had been for years. Perhaps there was something in Strang's past catching up with him. Most of the saliant developments in the ex-rancher's career were noted down in one section or another, but the entries which most interested Slim harked back to the worthy man's early days.

For the first time, Slim realised that Jason had been brought up in Kansas City. He was an orphan raised by a couple as their own eldest son before they started a family of their own. While still in his early teens, Jason had run away from home and taken up with pioneers moving west.

His brief entries suggested that Ma Ferris and her husband did not always get on well together. 'Bull', the husband, worked in a mine. He did not like the work, and often he was liquored up when he could afford it. When in liquor he was bad to deal with. Moreover, he resented Jason, and often walloped him. This was why the boy left home. Some time after he had started his travels, Bull's employer's mine petered out, and left Ferris without work. This made life very difficult for Ma, until the Civil War drew Bull away from her. He had left her with one small child. Others, boys, were born at intervals. Clearly, the Ferris family had never prospered, after Jason left them. He appeared to have somehow acquired a useful working knowledge of their goings-on, but had made no attempt to go back there, or to put them on their feet in New Mexico, where he had settled down.

There were gaps in the diary. Often as long as half a year had no entries at all. But Slim felt that he had come upon a possible source of hatred. Maybe some of the Ferris family were plotting Strang's downfall. He wondered if he had already met any of them in his travels.

10

In the peace office of San Juan, a swarthy-skinned deputy was leaning forward from the hips and peering through the dirt-stained window up the street. Presently, during the second hour of the afternoon, a man on horseback increased his interest.

He cleared his throat, blew aside his rather tatty moustache and talked out of the side of his mouth to the town marshal who was folded down in his chair with his elbows planted wide apart on the desk.

'Marshal, that fellow is comin' down the street, the one who came in from Texas to work for Strang. Wouldn't it be a good idea to talk with him?'

'You think so, Alfonso?' Marshal Grain queried, all the while exploring his pockmarked face with nervous fingertips.

The Mexican deputy nodded very decidedly. 'He is not the man Jason Strang is. I think I would talk to him, show the town that this office still has a lot of authority.'

Grain cleared his throat, rose from his chair and reached for his hat. The old army discipline put a straightener in his back as he limped for the street door and threw it open. Out on the sidewalk, he adjusted the pointed brim of his stetson and looked around for Blake.

Slim was twenty yards away and still coming closer. He had a far-away look in his eye, and reacted with a sudden start when Grain called to him. Automatically, he angled the dun across the street and headed for the boardwalk in front of the office. Grain was tall, and the sidewalk made him seem taller.

'Mr Blake, I believe you are resident in Mr Strang's house at this moment.'

'Marshal Grain, you are absolutely right. What can I do for you? Did you leave something behind?'

The marshal's expression became

fixed. On either side of him, strolling men and women, oblivious to the heat of the day, slowed to witness this exchange between the town marshal and this young fellow employed by Strang, who had made himself scarce.

'People often fight shy of talkin' to me about important town business, Mr Blake. I've heard tell that Mr Strang is out of town. If the eventuality should arise that I have to call him to the court house, I'd hate for him to be missin'. Do you follow me?'

'I follow you all right, Marshal. You want to hit a man when you think he's down. Jason Strang doesn't need to ask your permission to come and go. If he has any charge to answer, he'll be around. Maybe I could offer you a word of advice. Mind you don't go backing the wrong team, if there's goin' to be any sort of a showdown. Could be you won't be elected again, if you do.'

The dun shook its head and neck, and Grain had to step aside to avoid it. Slim touched his hat politely, and prepared to move on again. He called over his shoulder that Amos, the servant, would take any message if there was anything of interest while he, Blake, was away from the house.

Marshal Grain declined to answer, even by a nod.

★   ★   ★

In the slightly larger town of Las Vegas, it was the custom for many more of the townsfolk to rest in the heat of the day. However, the populace was on the move again by the time the dun carried Slim along the neat and imposing false fronts of Main Street, in what claimed to be the longest old town in the county. He found the sign denoting the *Las Vegas Chronicle* on the west side of an intersection between Main and First Avenue.

The dun was no more than a couple of yards away from the hitching rail and a tempting water trough when a tall, flamboyant figure came out from the front office door and halted on the sidewalk while he pushed long elegant fingers into a pair of light-coloured leather gloves.

Harman Grise, the owner, frowned when he saw that Slim was determined to speak to him. He shifted his feet for a moment, tapping with the end of his walking cane upon the worn boards beneath him. Grise was lean, and rather pompous in manner. His grey tuft of beard and waxed moustache were trimmed daily. Under the coat of his dark suit, a neat grey vest and a shirt with a winged collar were visible.

'Well, young man, what can I do for you? My time is precious. I'm a newspaper man, and to such as I, time is money.'

'Good day to you, Mr Grise, I hadn't thought to detain you. I know publication day has gone by for this week. All I wanted was to talk to someone who has the handling of submitted articles. I collect original drafts, often by famous authors and journalists.'

Slim had done his homework about who owned the paper, but the idea of representing himself as a collector of some sort had occurred to him on the spur of the moment. Grise studied him, touched his beard with the knob of his cane, and then seemed to come to a decision.

'All right, young man, you can go in. My editor is away, takin' a few days' leave. There's jest one employee in there, but he can show you any old manuscripts we've finished with. We don't have any special use for them, you understand. Only for back numbers of the newspaper. I'll say good day to you then.'

And with that, Harman Grise went off down the sidewalk with never a backward glance towards the site of his establishment. Slim slumped in the saddle for upwards of a minute. When he set out, it had seemed a fruitful thing to do, make a visit to the office of the newspaper which published a lot of

Jason's work. This could be the place where someone might have acquired copies of his handwriting, in order to perpetrate a forgery.

But now he had learned that the editor was away. Only a printer on the premises. Slim had no great opinion of printers. He was thinking rather pessimistically that his luck was probably out again.

The printer in question, when he hobbled into view in flat, buckled shoes, was not the sort of man to put a lot of confidence into a newcomer. His jeans were untidily tied with a thin cord at the waist, around a small paunch. The fellow wore a collarless shirt over a thick chest and stooping shoulders. His backbone was almost hunched. Fair, straw-coloured hair was pushed forward onto his forehead. Due to his stoop, he peered up at people from under rather heavy brows topped by a bony-looking cranium.

He rubbed his face with the back of his hand, having emerged from a rear room into the main part of the building. The printing press partially hid him from view.

'What can I do for you, mister? The Boss has jest gone out.'

'Mr Grise said you'd help me, so I'll step inside. Could you come around here, and perhaps talk to me in the office?'

The printer sighed. He licked his lower, protruding lip, as though he was thirsty. 'Don't know what you'd want to talk to me about, but I suppose no harm can be done. I'll be with you in a minute, if you'll go in.'

Slim nodded, and turned away to the door on his left, which gave access to the editorial office. Presently, the printer came back from the rear smelling of whisky. He had taken a pull at a small bottle he had hidden back there. Again wiping the lower half of his face with the back of his hand, he donned a fairly clean apron, and sat down facing Slim on the opposite side of the editorial desk.

Slim offered him a small cigar, acquired when he bought others for Jason. The printer's thoughts were on drink, but he took the proffered smoke and soon sucked on it contentedly.

'I guess you don't entertain many visitors in here when the Boss and the editor are out. May I ask what your name is?' Slim began conversationally.

'I'm Den Ferris, but nobody ever asks about me. I only set up the type an' work the presses. I'm a nobody, mister, and that's for sure.'

Ferris said it as though he meant it, but as soon as he had uttered his name, Slim was interested. Here, so soon after it had cropped up in Jason's diary, was the name of the family which had brought Strang up. Coincidence? More than likely. But, nevertheless, excitingly interesting.

Slim nodded and grinned. 'I only ever knew one lot of folks with the name of Ferris, an' they lived a long way from here. In Kansas City, to be exact. You wouldn't be related to Ma

Ferris who lives in that town, would you?'

Drink, and a somewhat debauched existence, had made Den Ferris act and look much older than his thirty years. Now, at the mention of his mother, a flicker of real life showed in his bloodshot eyes.

'My mother was the only Ferris woman in Kansas City, to my knowledge, mister, so I'd say you were talkin' about my kin. I been in these parts for quite a while now. Say, did you see Ma this year?'

Slim shook his head. 'No, but I think meetin' you calls for a celebration. Why don't we mosey off to the nearest saloon, where I can buy you a few drinks, while we talk? How would that be?'

Den appeared to be more secure within the confines of the newspaper building. He thought about the proposition for a long time, and then came up with a counter-suggestion. 'I have a bottle of whisky in the back room. I'll fetch it in here, an' we can drink that. Of course, if you wanted to give me the cash to buy the next bottle I wouldn't quarrel with you.'

Chuckling to himself, Slim dropped a silver dollar on the desk. He waited impatiently while Den Ferris came back with the half-bottle of whisky. After sharing a couple of drinks, he started to advance the conversation. After all, there was always a chance Grise might come back prematurely.

'Do you ever see Jason Strang when he calls in with articles, Den?'

The printer was mildly under the influence already, but the mention of Strang got through to him. He peered around his glass rather warily, and took a long time in deciding that his visitor did not know of any connection between Strang and himself.

'Most of the time I stay in the back room. Jest occasionally, I catch a glimpse of the contributors, but, like I said, I'm small fry around here.'

Slim moved his chair so that Ferris

could not fail to look him in the face. He said rather deliberately: 'Den, somebody's about to try an' take Strang's fortune away from him. In order to do it, they have to perpetrate a forgery. And in order to do that, they have to get their hands on several pieces of his handwriting.'

Slim stopped talking, and the wheezy breathing of the printer filled the rather dusty room. He was slow to answer. 'It's interesting, Mr . . . '

'Slim Blake. I am livin' in the Strang house in San Juan when my work isn't too pressin', Den. I'm employed as a private detective by Jason.'

'If you are a detective, why do you come here, Mr Blake?'

'This is a good place to come to, Den. After all, you grew up in the same house as Jason. An' you're in these parts, like he is. You know about him, what he does these days. Besides, you're in a position to get your hands on his articles, samples of handwriting, if anyone should want to borrow such things.'

Ferris' breathing remained slightly harsh, but he appeared to be sobering up. 'All right, so my Ma brought him up, but that don't mean I want his money. I'm no forger, if that's who you're lookin' for! An' if you'll take my advice, you'll leave pretty darned soon, mister, 'cause I've made up my mind I don't like private detectives!'

Ferris half-rose to his feet, gestured towards the door and waited for Slim to go. He was disappointed. To cover the interval, the printer tilted the bottle, pouring another finger of whisky into his glass.

When Slim eventually stood up to go, he did it very deliberately. In the doorway, he turned back and said: 'So you don't know anything about Strang's trouble at all, eh? That means you are leavin' Edith to take the punishment for the crime on her own! Well, that's about what I'd expect from a Ferris. Adios. I won't trouble you again.'

Slim purposely got as far as the outside door before he allowed Ferris to overtake him. The bloodshot eyes were haunted as the pitiful man interposed himself between Slim and the outer door.

'What was that you said about Edie?'

'She may have to take the punishment on her own.'

Ferris sagged against the door, blocking the point of exit. He wanted to ask for confirmation, for proof that Edie was in trouble, but his morale was low, and Slim could see that.

'Forgery leadin' to a kind of fraud. Jason could put her away for a long time, if we manage to prove what she's done. A pity such a pretty forger as that should have to malinger in jail. The jury won't like it, but they'll have to do their duty, though.'

Ferris waxed almost eloquent in a pathetic sort of way. 'Mister, Edie ain't no forger. She's a fine girl. Although she's only a second cousin to me, she's more like a daughter to my Ma. Any time Ma was hard-pressed, if she could contact Edie she'd get relief. Edie was never tight with her money, like some folks I know. Leave her be. Look somewhere else for the criminal, will you?'

'But Edie is right there, in San Juan, tellin' all the townsfolk that Jason offered her marriage and she accepted. She's askin' for a whole heap of trouble. I don't see how anyone can do anything for her, now that she's so deeply involved. Another thing puzzles me. Jason talked to me about her before I ever met her. But he never said she was any sort of kin to the folks who reared him.'

'She wouldn't, mister. Because you see, Jason had run away from home by the time Edie was a babe-in-arms in the next valley. They never knew each other back in Kansas. That's the way it was. I wish it was jest like that now.'

Slim's mind was very active. He eased Ferris aside and stepped out onto the sidewalk. The worried printer followed him.

'All the trouble is in San Juan,' Slim

repeated. 'I have Jason hidden away at Bobcat's Retreat, but all this will have to come to a head if Edie insists on a court action. And what's more, Jason sure can be vindictive. When he finds out the link between Edie an' your Ma, he might strike out for revenge, thinkin' your Ma put her up to what she's doin'.'

Ferris laid a hand on his arm, as though to detain him further, but Slim, having planted a lot of ideas in the poor fellow's head, wanted to get away now and await developments. He put the fellow firmly aside, hurried back to his mount and swung up into leather.

'It's been good to talk to you, Den. A pity we didn't have a happier subject to talk about.'

Touching his hat, Slim sent the dun down the street, in the direction by which it had arrived. He thought that Den was sufficiently troubled to pay somebody a call: either in San Juan or Bobcat's Retreat. Whichever he chose,

Slim felt certain that Strang was going to be better off. Den was a weak character, and, in order to protect Jason, his weakness could be exploited.

11

Edie Lamont, around the time when Slim was leaving Las Vegas, was in a very restless and uncertain frame of mind. She was strolling around her hotel room in a pair of denim levis and a faded man's blue shirt with pleated pockets over her breasts.

She had been in a position to show the world a sophisticated exterior for upwards of half a dozen years. But she never forgot her humble origins. At times of stress, she pulled out the outfit which she was now wearing and marvelled at the changes which had occurred in her life since she had left the derelict Lamont homestead in the valley wide of Kansas City.

In her youth, she had behaved like a boy. Even now, she had habits which would be considered way out in a respectable young woman of modest means. For instance, she could smoke a mild cigar alongside of any man. She glanced at her reflection in a long mirror attached to the portable wardrobe, and frowned. From the depths of her valise, under the bed, she extracted a cigar from a small leather container.

She lit it with a flourish, and sucked smoke down into her lungs, leaving a faint trace of lipstick around the weed, near the tip.

Edie was worried. She had nerve, lots of it, and she had never hesitated to put herself out on a limb for a friend or relation. On this occasion, the limb she was out on was substantial. And the man involved with her had a reputation as a great fighter. Jason Strang would fight back, and no mistake. Besides, he had that handsome young detective, Slim Blake, researching for him all the time, and Slim had plenty of sand in his craw, too.

If only the Ferris boys had been as courageous as Slim, she would not be in her present predicament. She stopped pacing by the window and glanced down into the street. A mild breeze touched her hair, reminding her that it was still piled up on the top of her head. In the days when she had worn the rougher man-like gear, it had been tied at the nape of her neck.

Screwing her eyes to miss the cigar smoke, she stepped to the wardrobe mirror and pulled out the pins which secured her hair, one by one. Down it came in a rich becoming copper bell, about her shoulders, appearing to make her face narrower. Even the lines of her face, which were few and almost invisible, seemed changed by the new hair style. She saw herself as more wistful, effeminate. The girl she would have liked to be, if life had not dealt quite so harshly with her.

She examined the tip of the cigar rather critically, but came to no conclusion about it, except that the ash was getting long. She had friends, particularly in Pueblo. They wouldn't turn against her, but they would forget her if she started to live for any length of time in another place.

Here in San Juan, the men who approached her were really only admirers, this far. She had seen one or two to whom she felt she could apply for a little sympathetic aid, if circumstances went against. But no one she would like to take on for life. Not yet.

Still, she had a little time in hand. Time, the great enemy, had not reduced her chances among the wealthy and eligible men who admired her.

Quite abruptly, her thoughts turned to the cousins, the Ferris family, and the sad state their lives were in. She supposed that they had inherited some sort of character weakness through Bull, the father. Poor Den had been the oldest. He had tried any one of several jobs in and around Kansas City, for his mother's sake, and got himself a reputation for being unreliable.

He had been the first of the Ferris boys to be sent west to contact Jason Strang, as a last chance to make good.

Undoubtedly, Jason had tried to help Den. He had managed to get him a position in a bank, through his undoubted influence. Drink, a loose tongue, and a chronic inability to calculate with any accuracy had resulted in Den being dismissed and Jason Strang having a bad quarrel with his bank manager.

After that, Den had been given a chance on the Box J. But not as an honoured relation. Den had to bunk in with the boys, and find himself a useful job to do around the spread. Ranch work was one form of employment which none of the Ferris boys was cut out for. The nearest they ever got to punching cows and like occupations was in riding trail horses.

Den had failed on the spread, been given a small sum to set him up elsewhere, and then told to go. Jason had washed his hands of him. Den had drifted for a time. He had had the good sense not to trouble Jason any more. Eventually, he had fallen into the job of printer's handyman at the offices of the Las Vegas newspaper.

A man almost in his dotage had taught him how to set up type, and then had died, creating a semi-permanent opening for Den at a time when his employer was thinking of getting rid of him. Any spare money which Den had went on the bottle. He never had enough to send any home to his mother who was permanently short. But he still loved his mother, and he knew that Edie was good to Ma Ferris. For this, Den was devoted to Edie for as long as he remained sober.

Poor Den. The seal was set upon his unhappy life because of the drink, and his weakness of character. The woman did not exist who could pull him out of his path of self-destruction.

Grimacing rather bitterly, Edie rubbed out the cigar and tossed the but out of the window. She caught another glimpse of herself in the mirror, and for once she did not like what she saw. She sat down on the bed, and tied her hair with a piece of yellow ribbon.

Her own career had been a varied one. First, she had worked to give herself an education of sorts. Within three years of her own studies having started, she was employed for short hours transmitting reading, writing and arithmetic to the children of those less well endowed who could not send them to a proper schoolmistress.

That crucial year came when she managed to leave home and try for jobs in town. She had danced, sung and acted as a croupier in a succession of places where the management had taken her on for her good looks, tired of being held at arm's length by her, and then kept her on because of her undoubted brain power in an atmosphere where mistakes were made and funds often lost.

The ability to calculate had made it possible for her to work behind the counter in shops. In that sort of work she had learned to keep accounts. Keeping accounts had been the groundwork for office work of one kind or another, and her grooming, learned on the way, had caused men with professional offices to employ her. By way of a change, she had sometimes worked as the travelling bookkeeper for neighbouring ranches.

Sometimes the ranchers' wives had looked askance at her, wondering if she was unduly interested in their husbands, or their sons, seeing that she came to live in their houses when the accounting was being done. But she had given them no special cause for concern, and she only left when she became bored, or when trouble was about to rear its head.

Before this, she had always shied away from trouble. What she was doing here in San Juan was almost out of character.

Over the years, she had earned a lot of money. Most of it had been spent. But not all of it. At frequent intervals, amounts like fifty dollars, and sometimes one hundred dollars, had found their way to the Ferris family in their shack near Kansas City.

Edie had never begrudged her weak aunt's calls upon her in times of stress. Aunt Ferris had always been kind to her when she was a girl. It was knowing that Jason, a man who had grown up in the Ferris household, withheld money from Mr Ferris which made Edie bitter enough to take action against him. He had enough funds to set up the whole Ferris family and then have enough left over to live comfortably for the rest of his life.

Jason had ample funds, and Mr Ferris was destitute. Edie never forgot this. Just the same, she was sober-minded enough to know that she had put herself into a very difficult position on Ma Ferris' behalf. If things went against her, she might even end up in prison. And that surely would be a change for the worse.

Men had glanced after her and admired her for many years now. None of them, however, would go against the findings of a court, should the present dilemma come to that and the result go against her.

Would Jason soften when he found out the connection between the two of them? It was unlikely. After all, another of the Ferris boys had been through for help since Den. This one, Rick, had been helped into work with a wagon train. His character weakness had made him quit the train at a critical time, stealing two of the best horses when they could ill be spared.

And then there was Lefty, the third Ferris brother. He had not been New Mexico way, but it had been rumoured in certain quarters that he had hit the owlhoot trail. Jason, if he was at all interested, probably knew about that, too. He would not hand out any favours to a girl who was a blood relation of theirs.

Moreover, he had already shown himself to be impervious to all her womanly wiles. How would it be if, when the crunch came, her many would-be friends turned aside from her? Where would she turn, if Jason lived out her bluff, up to the end of the month, and then bested her in court? There was always a chance he might do that. Slim Blake could be the turning point He could give evidence about a known thief, Derby Jones, coming out of her home in Pueblo at a time when Slim had been lured out of town.

He might even locate Den. If he did that, then Edie would be in dire trouble. Den was devoted to her, but he could never keep them out of trouble, if pressure was put upon him.

She rose to her feet, eyed herself in the mirror, and speculated. How would it be if she made herself the plaything of some rich man, and let life do what it could to her after that? She had never degraded herself in that way before, and she never seriously considered it now. How could she when she was posing as Jason's fiancée? Besides, Jason was the only man with the means and the intelligence to put himself into the category she was thinking about, and he was indifferent to her.

She thought that perhaps she could try her best feminine tricks on Slim Blake. He could be impressed by a pretty woman. She had known this as early as their first meeting in Pueblo. But where would it get her, if she succeeded in influencing him? Would he go against his client's best interests, for her sake? She did not know. Nor did she want to find out. If he could be corrupted, then he was not up to much, as far as his character was concerned.

With an effort, she managed to shrug away for a time her pressing doubts. An earlier idea had been a better one. She would seek employment. If public confidence went against her, it would look well if she was doing a useful job. She would go out looking her best and seek employment. Already, she knew what sort of employment she wanted. It was bookkeeping work for ranchers in the South Creek Basin. She knew also the men she wanted to approach.

★ ★ ★

Wayne Malloy and Sam Wardle were at their favourite table in the saloon when Edith Lamont looked in rather cautiously. She saw that they were present, and went so far as to nod and smile in their direction, but she withdrew, and it was a tiny nondescript man off the street who brought to them the message that Miss Lamont would like to talk to them on a business matter.

The ranchers promptly stood up and prepared to follow the messenger to the nearby café where Miss Lamont was supposed to be waiting for them. They looked eager. In and around the town, Malloy's wife, Brigid, was nicknamed 'Frigid', and it was common knowledge that Mrs Wardle had allowed herself to grow fat and coarse through pressures of childbirth.

Edith had made her choice well. She had chosen two men who were opposed to Jason Strang and his interests; two men who, at the same time, had reasons for seeing the attractive woman in her. Each of them would make excuses in order to employ her, though they had got along without the services of a bookkeeper for many years, and always previously made it known that they could not afford one.

Dire need made her show her personality to the best advantage as they walked slowly past the windows of the café, eyeing her all the way to the door.

12

Lefty Ferris, a younger brother of Den who worked for the *Las Vegas Chronicle*, was a vicious, restless individual with habits that drew attention to himself, and the other men who happened to be riding with him at the time. This tendency to attract publicity was not favoured among intelligent outlaws.

Lefty had ridden with his two present partners for several months, on and off, but during a recent period when they had been separated for a while, he had ridden into an isolated ranch house in the next county further west and roughed up the family to such an extent that one or two very determined lawmen were attempting to find him over a large piece of territory.

Moreover, they had a passing useful description of him, and he knew about this. They were looking for a dark-haired youngish man with a drooping black moustache who favoured his left hand when it came to using weapons. As he rode towards Las Vegas for the purpose of talking with his down-trodden brother, Lefty fingered his freshly scraped upper lip where the moustache had been. He was wondering if the light, bare patch of skin would give away the fact that he had shaved off his moustache. He always favoured his left hand when it came to guns, and he could not do anything about that. He found himself shrugging, as his strong pinto carried him into the north-western outskirts of Las Vegas. One of the local peace officers was related to another who had chased him further west, but, with a little luck, no one would see him, or tie him in with the nameless wanted man he had become.

Just short of the nearest building, Lefty slid to the ground and from that point he walked his horse towards the rear side of the newspaper building. The light was rapidly fading, and lamps were lit in several dwellings ahead of him. The rear of the *Chronicle* building had been extended at one time, so that two extra rooms could be added. Den Ferris lived in a small box-like one-room building which stood just clear of the extensions.

A lamp was burning in Den's place, whereas the bigger building beside his was in darkness. Lefty began to feel more at ease, as he got his bearings. He tied up the pinto in the alley between two of the larger edifices and quietly knocked on Den's door.

No answer came from within. Lefty knocked again, without response. Then, after cautiously peering around him in all directions to make sure that he was not being watched, he grasped the door handle, pushed it open and stepped inside.

His brother was there all right. Slumped with his head on the centrally-placed small wooden table in an attitude of sleep. The aroma of whisky filled the room. An empty bottle lay on its side on the table. It wobbled as Lefty's feet moved over the worn floorboards. To one side was a bunk bed, still ruffled from the previous evening. Dirty dishes were stacked on a bench. Discarded clothing hung on two nails on either side of a window.

The atmosphere was stale. Lefty frowned. He straightened up, moved around to the window, where he fixed an old drape across the glass, and then lit for himself a home-rolled cigarette. Then, and only then, did he move back to his brother and attempt to rouse him.

'Hey, Den, rouse up, will you? This is Lefty, your brother, talkin'. I came a long way jest to talk to you about the future. So shake yourself and show a bit of interest.'

Den snored on, dribbling a little at the mouth. Lefty punched his shoulder without any marked result. Suddenly the visitor's temper flared. He pushed his burning cigarette end close under his brother's nose and brought it away quite slowly. The hairs in Den's nose singed. He sniffed, shook himself and tried to rouse himself.

'What — what in tarnation happened to my nose?' he grumbled.

He touched it, sniffing the burning in his own nostrils. He blinked hard and his eyes opened. He saw the figure of his brother standing across the room from him with a half-full pitcher of water in his hand.

'Are you thirsty, big brother?' Lefty jeered.

'I'm always thirsty, an' Edie is in trouble. You *are* Lefty, ain't you? The light is bad, an' you're standin' in the shadow. I seem to see you without a moustache. Have you shaved it off? What did you do to my nose?'

'I took off the moustache 'cause I didn't like carryin' it around any more, brother. Your nose was a little singed because I couldn't rouse you an' I don't have a lot of time to talk.'

Without any warning, he tossed the water over Den, who edged back on his stool and shook his head. His loose underlip undulated as he caught his breath and glared at the unfeeling figure of his younger, wayward brother.

'My bottle is empty, Lefty, I don't have anything to offer you.'

Ignoring the note of supplication in Den's voice, Lefty pulled up another stool and fixed him with an unwavering glance. 'I don't want liquor. All I want is advice from you. Now, are you sober enough to listen for a while?'

'Unfortunately, yes. But I can't think what a rip-roarin' young galoot like you would want to learn from me. You'd do better to buy a copy of the paper. Me, I can't remember anything, not even after I've set it up in print. But ask on, I'll try to answer you.'

Lefty fingered his short upper lip. He gave a brief smile, in the hope of improving Den's attitude towards him. In this, he failed. Den knew him well. Lefty was only here to better his own position, probably at the expense of some innocent.

'I heard tell in my travels that Edie Lamont was this way, and that there were easy pickings to be had in San Juan. Somehow or another, Edie was mixed up with a wealthy man. Is that right?'

Den's brow furrowed a little more deeply. He scratched the hair growing around his prominent breastbone. 'Edie is in trouble. She's tryin' to hold Jason Strang to an offer of marriage which he didn't make. I think she might have to go to prison.'

Lefty removed his smoke from his mouth. His short upper lip moved above prominent front teeth which were yellowing.

'You say she's aimin' to marry Jason Strang?' he repeated. 'Can't say that's like Cousin Edie, but she sure has nerve. Maybe I've underestimated her all these years. Why is she doin' it? Is she tired of bein' poor?'

'She's doin' it for our Ma, to try an'

get a whole lot of money out of Jason, who never sent her anything, not even when she was really hard up. But it won't work. In a few days she'll have to take Jason to court. *I* think she'll lose the case, not win it. If she loses, she'll have to go to jail for fraud, and maybe some other sort of offence to do with blackenin' Jason's character.'

'You really think Strang can put her in jail, brother?'

'I certainly do, Lefty. Edie, she's a good girl. She needs protection. She's workin' for our Ma, but Ma wouldn't want her to go to jail, if things went wrong.'

Lefty's frown of perplexity slowly left his face. It was replaced by a smile, which did little to warm the atmosphere. He smiled for the wrong sort of reasons.

'Maybe it's a good thing I happened along when I did, Den. *I*'m the one to help Edie. And I don't have anything more pressin' to do right now. Where can I find Strang? He will have to be worked over a little, but when I've finished with him he won't consider takin' Edie to court over anything.'

'Edie is the one who has to bring the matter to court, Lefty. You don't understand. If she backs down now, she'll lay herself open to charges. Besides, Jason Strang ain't at his home. He's gone into hidin'.'

Lefty's enthusiasm ebbed, but his brain went on working with the problem. 'Not many people will know about Jason goin' into hidin'. If *you* know, maybe you know where he went.'

'Some place called Bobcat's Retreat, I guess. The detective said he'd gone there until all the fuss was over. At least, I think that's what he said. This retreat would take a lot of finding. But it has to be a mile or two outside of San Juan. That's the town where Strang lives, and where Edie is now.'

Lefty beamed again. He started to get restless, rising to his feet and trying to peer past the drape at the window. To his surprise, Den rose, almost as

191

quickly. A restraining arm made Lefty look down.

'Lefty, if you go lookin' for Strang, promise me you'll stay away from Edie. She has enough trouble. If you went near her you'd only make things worse than what they are for her. Do you understand?'

Lefty was to resent this suggestion later. Just now he felt he knew what he had to do. He said things to placate his frightened brother and told him also to stay put, not to embarrass Edie by anything he did.

His last words were: 'Big brother, jest leave things to me. As you so rightly pointed out, it's a family matter. I wouldn't want to embarrass Edie any more than Ma would. So rest easy right here. Presently, the editor of your newspaper will get details of what's happened. You'll see that everything has turned out for the best.

'Here's a dollar to quench your thirst. Drink deep, an' forget I called on you, huh? Adios.'

Den hurried after him to emphasise the danger to Edie, but he was too late. Lefty had gone.

★   ★   ★

In the open, wide of Las Vegas, Willie Marvin and Roscoe Teal showed commendable vigilance as the single rider came towards their night camp. One man wriggled away from the fire and positioned himself behind the bole of a tree, while the other one went in the opposite direction and holed up in a shallow ditch.

'Howdy, boys, I can see you ain't asleep,' Lefty called. 'Sure is touchin' to have you wait up for me. You'll be glad you did, 'cause I've brought interestin' news for you.'

Teal, the man in the ditch, rose to his feet with a sour expression on his thin, swarthy countenance. The front of his black shirt had become wet with stagnant water, picked up in the ditch. He moved hurriedly into the firelight and started to dry it. Flickering flames showed the anger in his rather flat features and cold baleful eyes. Beneath the grey stetson which adorned his head he wore his brown sideburns rather bushy. One of them helped to hide his missing left ear top, which had once been shot off in a gun fight.

'Gosh durn it, Lefty, you could have given us earlier warnin', then we wouldn't have needed to plunge into the dirt to make sure we weren't bein' jumped. You don't have enough feelin' for your pardners, an' that's for sure!'

Lefty chuckled as he watched Teal drying himself, but he made an effort to keep his merriment in check. Willie Marvin returned to the warm area making little sound. He was wearing a pair of plains mocassins. The latter was thirty-five years of age, a seasoned law-breaker, with a bald head, a Syrian nose and pronounced lantern jaw. A huge neutral-coloured stetson with a very wide brim hid the twinkle of amusement in his small blue eyes.

The newcomer rapidly unsaddled and prepared himself for a few hours' sleep. As he did so, his curious partners listened to what he had to say.

'My cousin, Edie Lamont, is in San Juan. But Jason Strang, the fellow she wants to put the bite on, has skipped out. Chances are she could end up in trouble, but this is a glorious opportunity for the three of us.'

Teal, lounging on one knee and squatting on his saddle, was sceptical. 'You mean this is a chance for us to get into trouble *with* her?'

Marvin, blessed with a poker face and a still tongue, said nothing. Not knowing how he felt about the business, Lefty had to work to keep the enthusiasm in his voice while he made his revelations.

'Jason Strang has gone into hiding, in a shack called Bobcat's Retreat. But nobody is supposed to know where he is. Maybe two people know beside me. I thought we ought to go along there an' kidnap him. We could hide him and put the screw on anyone who wanted him back for maybe a million dollars!'

Pessimistically, Teal, the leader of the outfit, put the proposition in a poor light. 'Maybe no one would want him back, have you thought of that? Besides, we'd have to have a go-between, if we were to send our ransom note into town.'

'Perhaps it wouldn't come to that,' Lefty argued. 'Could be that Jason don't trust banks. I know this, he don't trust many people. But I think we could find our go-between, if we needed one. There's a detective chap keepin' in touch with him, you see.'

Teal was about to ask where they should hide the kidnapped man, when Willie Marvin spoke up. 'I know where Bobcat's Retreat is. It's real close to Red Rock Canyon, an' that's a box! Maybe we could lose him in there while the negotiations are goin' on.'

After a short pause, Teal showed more enthusiasm. 'Okay, we'll give it a try. But we sleep a few hours before we go lookin' for him.'

Lefty went to sleep with something approaching a smile on his homely countenance.

13

At ten o'clock the following morning, San Juan's town marshal, Richard Grain, was on the point of leaving his office to take coffee in a place just down the street. Deputy Al Garcia had already put up his feet to rest them on the padded bed in the first cell when the office door opened and in walked a stranger.

Den Ferris had a worn jacket over his shabby shirt and pants. An old stetson with a wavy brim kept the sun out of his tired-looking eyes. He straightened up, put on a bold face and asked for the marshal.

Grain, behind his desk, with the star on his black vest quite prominent, gave him a strange look and slowly sank back into the chair which he had just vacated. Garcia was hidden from view by a blanket pinned across the bars of the cell, but he sat up in order to know what manner of man had entered the building.

'Marshal, I'd like for you to have pencil and paper ready, because I have a confession to make. What I have to say is kind of serious, so if you could arrange it that we wouldn't get interrupted, I'd be obliged.'

Den gave off a slight trace of body odour which did not endear him to the thirsty peace officer, but Grain was sufficiently curious to humour him for a few minutes, at least.

'May I ask who you are, an' what manner of a confession you want to make, mister? I ought to warn you not to waste this office's time. Me, and my assistants, we're busy men. We have a big job to do.'

Den made a big effort to sit down and compose his thoughts, the better to be able to deliver himself of his confession.

'My name is Den Ferris. Originally I came from Kansas, but what I have to tell you about is connected with this territory, so I assure you I won't be wastin' your time.

'My statement concerns Miss Edith Lamont and Mr Jason Strang.'

At this point, Marshal Grain's jaw dropped in surprise, and Deputy Garcia fell off the bench where he was resting his weighty carcase. The visitor, startled by the sudden noise from the unexpected place, glared at the pinned-up blanket until Garcia's bare head showed above it. Alfonso was prepared to forego his short rest now that he knew this decrepit fellow had news about Strang and the Lamont woman. He came out of the cell scratching his dark, kinky hair which had grey highlights in it.

Seated on a third chair, he toyed with his hat.

'You were sayin', Mr — er?' Grain murmured.

'Den Ferris. Edith Lamont is my cousin. She is a pleasant, talented an' attractive girl an' always she has tried to help my Ma who is located near Kansas City. But Ma has had a biggish family and none of us have been a whole lot of good for her. Me, I'm a shinin' example of how not to turn out as a son. But at least I'm here to try and do what is right by Edie.'

'An' what *is* right by Edie?' the marshal prompted. 'You haven't said yet what has happened.'

'Edie is trying to get a lot of money out of Jason Strang. She's pretending he made her a proposal of marriage, only he never did do that. Somehow Jason was liquored after they met in Pueblo, an' he don't remember what went on any too clearly. But he didn't propose marriage, 'cause Jason wouldn't make that kind of a mistake.'

Grain's eroded eyes were glowing. Garcia was silently fascinated by the revelations.

'You are suggesting that Miss Lamont is perpetratin' a fraud of some sort, and that Mr Strang is the innocent victim of that fraud?'

201

'That's what I'm tellin' you, Marshal, as sure as fate. Edie won't like me for what I'm doin' 'cause as like as not she's prepared to let the matter go to court. I don't want that because one of the letters, the important one, could be proved to be a forgery.

'I'm here to make sure that Edie don't get punished for that forgery. You see, I forged the letter myself. Me, Den Ferris. I work for the *Las Vegas Chronicle*. I've had access to written material done in Jason's hand for a long time. I've practised, an' now I'm pretty good at it.

'Now, if you've got all that down, Marshal, I'll sign it. Then maybe you can lock me up. I sure would like for you to go easy on Miss Edie.'

Marshal Grain was, indeed, up to date with his writings, but he felt that there was a lot more that could be learned from this frank criminal who only wanted to go to jail to protect a young woman the whole town had taken to its heart.

'Mr Ferris, you talk about Mr Strang as if you knew him, usin' his Christian name all the time. *Do* you, in fact, know him?'

'Oh, sure, I know him. Jason was brought up by my Ma. Only he ran away from home before my time. Still, my Ma and us folks, her descendants, know more or less what Jason is about. It ain't hard to keep track of a gent who's as well known as he is.'

Grain breathed hard, and nodded. Garcia, unable to keep quiet any longer, asked the next question.

'Was Miss Lamont by any chance reared in the house of your Ma?'

'No, she grew up a little distance away. Not far enough to be cut off from us, her nearest kin. But Jason never knew her in the early days. Edie is only about twenty-eight, I guess. She would be jest a baby when Jasy took off, an' he ain't been back to Kansas City, so far as I know. Not ever.'

Grain stood up, bare-headed, and read the remarkable confession which he had in his hands. He knew that almost everyone of any consequence in San Juan had hoped Strang would bite the dust over the Edith Lamont affair. Now, almost certainly, they would all be disappointed. And all because a down-at-heel newspaper employee didn't want the girl to go to jail for forgery. Grain was not quite sure of the outcome of the affair. He knew that Ferris and his confession were dynamite, and he intended to get some legal advice about them. For the present, Den's immediate needs could be dealt with.

He handed over a pen for the visitor to sign. Den did this with scrupulous care. Grain signed in a different place, and Garcia countersigned. The document went away into the top drawer.

'Let Mr Ferris choose his own cell, Alfonso. And get him anything he needs. I'm goin' to talk to Jefferson James, the lawyer.'

The marshal left the building. Den

declined to use the first cell, and eventually took one at the rear, opening off a narrow corridor. This one, Garcia assured him, got more fresh air in, and, being at the back, he could not be stared at by visitors to the office. Den entered the cell willingly enough. He gave orders for a good meal, a pint of beer and a chaser of whisky. Garcia himself went out to get it.

* * *

Jefferson James, one of two capable attorneys who resided in San Juan, was about to close up his office for an hour when Marshal Grain walked in upon him and asked him to settle back in his chair, so as to be able to take a shock or two.

James was a tall man of fifty years, with a squarish cut beard and moustache, both more grey than black. His shoulders were broad, and his dark business jacket had been tailored to accentuate them.

Grain sat down in the visitor's chair, a thing he had never done before without being asked. James wondered at his temerity, but kept silent. Life, he reflected, was full of surprises. No one ever fully knew another man: not in every detail. Perhaps there was a stronger man inside the one San Juan's townsfolk took to be their marshal.

'You look like a man who has something of importance to impart,' he murmured.

'I am. Strang never proposed marriage to the Lamont woman. I have a man in cells who has confessed to forging a letter connected with the faked proposal of marriage. It's jest another attempt to separate Jason from his money. I could have gone to another office, but I thought I might be doin' you a favour by comin' here. Some few days ago, I thought I saw the woman in question coming out of here. Am I right?'

James nodded. His eyes were round with surprise. A confession was a feather in the marshal's cap. A confession plus a prisoner, doubly so.

'Is there any doubt about the confession?'

'None. The Lamont woman, Jason Strang and the witness were all brought up in the same area. Related, too, except that Jason was an orphan, and merely adopted. Where is the Lamont girl now?'

'Out at one of the South Creek ranches doing accounting work, so I've heard. I haven't seen her recently. The end of the month is close, though. Two more days. I had expected her to come along here and give me instructions to bring a case against Strang. Now, I suppose, the boot is on the other foot. She'll want to drop out of circulation without any publicity, if that can be arranged.'

'Can't anything be done for her?' Grain queried.

'It all depends upon Strang now. He's out of town, but that young detective is about. He should know where to contact him. Perhaps Strang will be lenient about the girl. I know it's unlikely, but stranger things have happened in my experience. I'll walk along with you to your office. I must see that confession with my own eyes. Also the fellow who made it.

'After that, one or other of us must go along to the Strang house and talk to the detective. Shall we go?'

Grain was aware that James was treating him with slightly more respect than usual. This pleased him. He rose to his feet and turned and went through the door without giving the lawyer the chance to go first.

* * *

Half an hour later, they were admitted to Strang's house by Slim, who heard them out in turn. He was as surprised as each of them had been when they heard the news. Den had more guts than Slim had imagined. And Edie was up to her neck in a whole heap of trouble. More than she had had to face in the whole of her life.

He agreed to get in touch with Jason, but he could give no assurance as to his client's reaction to the startling news.

14

Lefty Ferris had a novel way of attracting Strang's attention when the trio went into the draw which housed Bobcat's old cabin in the dark hours of that night. He it was who suggested that they should lure him out by teasing his stallion, the big smoke-grey animal by which the ex-rancher set great store.

Roscoe Teal, sometimes called Ross by his partners, cared little for Lefty's petty acts of cruelty, but his plan on this occasion looked like bringing about the desired result, and so the ringleader went along with it.

Lefty took his time about his actions, as he always did when he was thoroughly enjoying himself. He took off one of his spurs and tied it to a length of thin cord. When he was sure that it would not come loose, he joined Teal in stalking the stallion, which was pegged out on a long rope.

Teal managed to get to the peg without unduly startling the grey, although it was awake and rather apprehensive of him. As soon as the peg and the rope were within his grasp, Teal signalled for Lefty to get on with his act. Ferris was not slow to begin. Whirling the cord around his head like a bolas, he let fly at the beast just as it rose up and caught it a painful blow on the flank.

The grey whinnied in pain, and sprang away from the direction of the trouble, breaking into a trot which was cut short when the rope caught around a tree bole. Fifty yards away, the lamp in Bobcat's hut was being turned up. Teal, hanging onto the rope, was aware of this, but Lefty continued what he had started as though he had all night in which to torment the stallion.

He moved in closer the second time, swinging the spur in a vertical circle around his extended arm. His teeth showed in a fixed grin as he studied the head and expression of the tormented animal. It dodged this way and that, but not with sufficient speed to avoid the spur wheel which flew towards its flank.

This time, the animal jumped on all four legs. It backed away, tugging at the rope, and then swung back in an arc which would have freed the rope from the fouling tree bole, but the manoeuvre was only half completed when Lefty attacked again. This time the cast was a different one. The spur flew over the stallion's back. It settled very quickly and flew downwards, hitting the beast in a sensitive place, once again.

The sudden whinny this time drew a shout of rage from the remote cabin. Jason Strang, who had hastily got up off his bunk, ran out of the door with a rifle in his hand. He turned to go down the draw to where the stallion was tethered among trees, but he never got there.

Willie Marvin, a superb shot with a thrown pebble, hit him at the back of the head with his first missile and dropped him senseless to the ground.

Jason blacked out at once. He was not to know it at that time, but many capable men had bitten the dust in the same way, put down by the skilful hands of Marvin, a man thought by many influential people to be dead and buried in the Texas Panhandle.

'I got him, boys,' Willie called out casually. 'Why don't you bring the stallion up this way while we take a look around. After all, Jason is a man of some consequence. He might jest have a thing or two on his shelves we could use on our journey.'

Reluctantly, Ferris gave over tormenting the stallion. He walked up to the shack on his own, leaving Teal to bring along the animal. He was in time to see Willie Marvin dump Jason's senseless body on the rough wooden bench beside the table. Strang's upper trunk flopped across the table top and threatened to up-end the table, but Willie pushed him back and saw that it did not happen.

Lefty sat down on a stool on the

other side of the table, wanting to be right in front of Jason when he recovered consciousness.

Teal found a bottle of spirits, and poured out a small quantity for each of them. He and his partners had drunk theirs when Strang showed the first signs of regaining his senses. He had a contusion on the back of his head. His hat had been knocked off. Marvin had left it in a corner.

Lefty went over and collected the hat. He returned to his seat and picked up the fourth glass of liquor. He held Jason's head in his arm and pushed the glass towards his mouth.

'Folks say he don't ever drink that sort of stuff,' Willie opined, from the doorway.

'I know,' Lefty agreed. 'But a man has to change his habits sometimes. It's for his own good, ain't it?'

Jason recovered quite quickly as the fiery liquid went through his teeth and burned his tongue. As soon as he realised what was happening, he blew the whisky out of his mouth and gave Ferris a small shower in so doing around the face and neck. Lefty wanted to jab him in the face with the glass, but Teal firmly denied him the privilege.

'You may hate him, Lefty, but he ain't rightly recovered yet from that blow on the head.'

Glowering with suppressed rage, Ferris let go of the head of the man he hated. Instead, he jammed the expensive undented stetson on the hurt skull with such force that Jason almost cried out with the pain engendered by the contusion. Teal and Marvin made no attempt to heighten the tension in the room, and Ferris backed off for a while.

'If you boys think you've got a prior claim to this shack, take it by all means. I'll move out,' Jason offered. 'There's no need to act mean about it, teasin' my hoss an' all that. What do you hope to get that you can't get by jest askin'?'

Lefty bubbled over with his own special type of mirth. 'Oh, you sure said something that time, Jason. You sure did. When we go, you're goin' with us, an' we ain't plannin' to take our eyes offen you until a considerable portion of your fortune is in our possession. How does that strike you?'

Strang sniffed and massaged his moustache with the back of his hand. His gaze went to Lefty's pale upper lip. Suddenly he smiled. 'You gave me the answer I expected. So what are we waitin' for? You, there, with the short upper lip, you're a Ferris, one who didn't come beggin' to me. But you're not a beggar, you're a taker. Did Edie put you onto me?'

'Cousin Edie? Why no, Jason. To tell you the truth, I ain't set eyes on Cousin Edie this trip. I been in touch with my brother, Den, that's all.'

The sudden knowledge that Edith Lamont was a cousin to the Ferris family shocked Jason far more than the threat of kidnap and ransom. He blinked a lot, but tried hard to hide his surprise. Lefty did not notice why he was acting in the way he did.

Teal then spoke up. 'I hope you won't take it badly when I tell you we're goin' to hold you in Red Rock Canyon, Mr Strang?'

Jason turned, in his gaze acknowledging Teal as the leader. He nodded, glanced closely at Willie Marvin, and finally expressed his opinion. 'I guess I'd take my victim to the same place, if I was wearin' your boots. But I can tell you this, whatever happens to me, I won't tell you whereabouts in my house my savings are hid. So don't waste your time by puttin' Lefty, here, up to any fancy tricks.'

'We thought you might leave a note namin' the ransom price, before we left,' Marvin murmured. He was talking round a chewed matchstick.

This remark was unrehearsed, but Teal let it ride. He raised his brows, glanced across at the glowering Ferris boy, and was pleased when Strang asked for pencil and paper. Teal dictated the message; only the amount of the ransom money caused surprise.

To Slim Blake, or anyone visiting this cabin.

Jason Strang, a townsman of San Juan, is being held captive against his will. Only one thing will ensure his safe release. The arrival in Red Rock Canyon of one hundred thousand dollars in coin and easily negotiable notes. Mind how you come, or Strang will die.

'All right, so there's your ransom note. I'll sign it now,' Jason offered. 'What makes you think anyone will take notice of it?'

Marvin remained poker-faced over this query. Ferris glowered, but Teal answered. 'Instinct tells me, Mr Strang. I have a feelin' the note will prove popular.'

Five minutes later, captors and captive were riding out of the draw on the way to Red Rock Canyon. Marvin had taken it upon himself to guide them.

218

At dark the journey to the entrance to the box canyon took two hours. By the time that Willie called back that they had gone far enough, the prisoner and the two other captors were all in a rebellious mood. Somehow, the towering cliff-like walls on either side of the entrance repelled the humans. No one wanted to go forward into the inky blackness of the canyon floor.

Strang, stripped of all obvious weapons, moved about collecting firewood along with the others. Teal and Marvin were dubious about him for a time, but when he produced a match and ignited the fire, they began to think that he had accepted the inevitable. They felt sure that he would not try anything.

Ferris busied himself with the coffee pot and the frying pan. Everyone had taken a drink of coffee when Strang intimated that he wanted to answer a call of nature. Ferris looked as though he was about to follow him, so he protested, and Teal gestured for Lefty to stay back.

'Jest make sure he gets back, Lefty. That's all I expect of you.'

Ferris glowered and fumed, but he stayed away from the big rock behind which Strang went to relieve himself. For a time, the undented stetson bobbed down behind the highest point, then it showed again. The trio were beginning to think that Strang could hold an awful lot of liquid when the sound they had been listening to stopped.

Lefty suddenly darted around the rock and snatched up the big coffee mug. It had been gradually emptying itself while they listened. Moreover, the black felt stetson was still there, perched on the top of the rock. Jason had bolted. The trio of men were shaken. They fired off shots in several directions, aimed above the level of his head. But they heard no noises.

'You two fools are to blame for this,' Lefty blustered. 'You always thought you were cleverer than me, jest because I show my feelings. Now we've lost the key to a hundred thousand dollars. What are you proposin' to do now, Boss?'

This last question was directed to Teal, of course. The leader massaged the flat top of his misshapen ear, a habit he indulged in when he was nonplussed. His senses were still on the alert, however, and he showed this by bending down at the fire and snatching out a burning brand.

'Here, take this. Get over in that direction an' light another fire. We have to make sure he stays on that side of us, understand? He has to be still on the canyon side when daylight comes. If we fix that, there's no great harm done.'

Lefty took the burning twig and went off to do Teal's bidding. A well-aimed stone rattled his left boot as he thrust the brand into a clump of tumbleweed to start the second blaze. He turned, straightened up and blasted off two shots, but Strang failed to give away his position. Marvin, fire-lighting on the other flank, had a similar experience, but he did not react by using his gun. He had the best night vision of the three, and he knew that if anyone glimpsed Strang it was likely to be himself.

The three fires had the desired effect. It was almost impossible for Strang, or indeed for anyone, to crawl through the line of three guns to double back in the opposite direction. Jason, beyond their line of vision, accepted the situation philosophically. Even with daylight, he felt that all need not be lost. He could afford to wait. If they wanted him in a hurry, they would have to hunt him, and that would not be easy.

★ ★ ★

An hour before dawn, the tired watchers held a council of war. The outcome changed things. The man with the best night vision, Willie, remained on guard at the canyon mouth. He retained quite a lot of the stores which they had brought along with them.

Teal and Ferris, having assumed that the note in Bobcat's shack might remain unobserved for some time, were going to make their way into town, on the off chance of being able to find Strang's fortune hidden in his house.

15

Slim had breakfast at eight o'clock that morning. He ate it in leisurely fashion, and saw to the saddling of two horses while Amos cleared up the breakfast things. Around a quarter to nine, detective and house servant went round to the stable and mounted up.

Slim was heading for Bobcat's Retreat, and Amos was taking the day off to visit an aged relative of his mother in Las Vegas. They shook hands before parting.

Although Slim had never seen the Retreat in daylight, he found it in a much shorter time than when he took Strang along at dark. He was full of optimism, following the startling development of the previous day when Den Ferris had made his confession. Slim would have felt far less confident and uplifted if he had known Roscoe Teal and Lefty Ferris had come along that way at an earlier hour.

As it was, his face was split almost from ear to ear with a wide smile when he sprang to the ground and raced into the wooden shack to give Jason the news. The first and most obvious thing he noticed was that Jason was absent. Secondly, he found the note awaiting him, and that sent his spirits down to zero.

No mention of who had done the kidnapping, of course. Only the brusque demand for a sum of money coming to six figures. Either someone was very greedy, or they had a good idea of what Strang was really worth.

Sitting on the edge of the table, Slim tried to readjust his thoughts to face the new emergency. He read again, '*Mind how you come, or Strang will die.*' He thought it was all grossly unfair. Just at a time when Jason's troubles were over, everything was going against him again. Without being fully aware of what he was doing, Slim walked out of the shack, mounted up and turned his dun towards Red Rock Canyon. Almost a furlong had gone by before he realised that he was doing his client no good. If the kidnappers were sufficiently desperate, then only the ransom money would preserve Jason's life. And he, Slim, was the only man to do the negotiating. No one else could be expected to act as a go-between for the kidnappers. Besides, he was on the payroll.

Arriving back at the shack, he stopped only to give himself a drink and to briefly rock the saddle. He then began the return ride to town at a slightly slower pace.

★   ★   ★

The news about the confession and the man who had made it was all over the town when Lefty and Teal arrived in the middle of the morning. They paused at a Mexican *cantina* long enough to drink a glass of wine, and to hear all the known facts. A change came

226

over Lefty when he knew that brother Den had given himself up to the town marshal. He was angry, though if anyone told him he had a sense of family honour, he would not have believed them.

Teal watched the change come over him, and wondered how Lefty would be affected by the news. Lefty began to breathe deeply. He was in the throes of deep emotion. He drew Teal aside.

'I want an hour to get my brother out of there. You understand, Ross?'

'I understand your brother's a fool, that you could be jeopardisin' a very lucrative job by goin' after him right now.'

'I won't jeopardise anything,' Lefty argued firmly. 'You take a look at the Strang place. I'll be along with you. I won't bring my brother along, either. So rest easy, Ross, an' trust me, huh?'

Teal maintained a poker expression on his face. The speed of his walk betrayed what he was feeling about this sudden change of plan when he left the *cantina* alone. Lefty grinned his short-lipped smile, and removed his presence from the drinking den a little more slowly.

He walked until he came across a series of shops, mostly general stores. When he saw the type he was looking for, he made a note of the place and then moved his horse onto open ground behind the peace office. There he tethered it. He hung around the rear of the building where Den was incarcerated long enough to hum and sing a song much favoured by their mother in the old days. He then made his way in a leisurely fashion to the rear of the shops he had spotted earlier.

After a time, he found a stores shed with the lock undone, and not far inside the door was what he sought. He appropriated the necessities and came out, anxious not to be seen. Fifty yards away, in a small hollow which was partly hidden on the waste ground by old packing cases discarded by the shops, he put down his miniature stick of dynamite and unravelled the long fuse which he had attached to it. Some fifty feet away, he put a match to the fuse.

His next movements were rather more positive. He hurried back to the rear of the peace office, gave a tap on the walls of the cell, and awaited developments. The explosion went up with a deep roar of sound. The old packing cases and showers of earth were scattered in all directions. Immediately following the big crash, the townsfolk were silent. But soon there was a reaction. Over and above the crackle of burning lumber, men appeared to be converging upon the scene of the explosion from all directions. Marshal Grain and his deputy were among the first to rush across the dirt street and disappear down a convenient alley.

By that time, Lefty, who was grinning broadly, had his back to the all-metal rear door of the peace office cell corridor. He was quite prepared to use an explosive again, but he did not think this would be necessary. He had in his possession three pieces of wire, all bent to different patterns. The second one which he inserted in the lock opened the door. That gave him access to the corridor.

Den started up, shaking his head, as he saw Lefty, but the latter went up the corridor on tiptoe, assured himself that no one was left in the office, and came back to try out his lock-picking talents on the door of the cell.

'I don't want to do it, Lefty. I have to stay here an' face what's comin' to me.'

Lefty chuckled rather coldly. As the door opened inwards, he remarked: 'Ma wouldn't be happy to hear you talkin' like that. Especially when I've gone to all this trouble to get you out. You goin' to let me down?'

The outlaw did not wait for an answer, but propelled his brother through the door and down the corridor. The doors were closed again. Out in the open air, Lefty led the way to where the restless pinto awaited them.

'I'm no horse rider,' Den protested again.

'You are today, but only for a few minutes. Up you go, boy.'

Lefty boosted him into the saddle and mounted up behind him before he could protest further. The pinto, carrying its double burden, nevertheless answered briskly when its master called for an effort. Out they went into another, lesser thoroughfare, where the two-tone horse went along at a useful pace. Only one slow-moving townsman of advanced years showed any interest in the double burden. Lefty slowed long enough to explain that he was taking his brother along to see a doctor. He knew a doctor lived in the direction that they were travelling.

Around another turning, Lefty dismounted, but insisted on Den remaining in the saddle. Den hung on with a bad grace, and examined every face as though he expected to be rearrested at any moment.

'Quit moanin' will you, brother? Ain't nobody in the town knows your face exceptin' them out of the peace office, and maybe that detective you talked about.'

Den could read the signs as well as anyone. He knew Lefty's temper was rising, so from then on he kept the peace. Across a yellow-grassed hollow just clear of the last buildings, Lefty hauled the pinto to a stop. When asked to dismount, Den removed himself clumsily and fell in a heap against his brother, who hauled him upright again.

'You see the direction I'm pointin' in? Mebbe three hundred yards down there you'll find a tame old mule staked out. Grab him and use him. He's saddled already. I saw him on the way into town. You are to continue in that direction. Stop for a rest at Bobcat's Retreat, then keep goin' on till you reach the mouth of Red Rock Canyon. Understand?'

Den understood, but was protesting

about the desirability of this course of action. His protests suddenly went feeble when Lefty grabbed him by the collar and twisted his shirt, so that he found it hard to breathe.

'Brother, you are pretty darned ungrateful to me for what I'm doin', but you're goin' to do as I say, jest the same. At the mouth of Red Rock Canyon, one of my buddies will stop you. Tell him who you are, an' everything will be all right. All you have to do is tell him you're Lefty's brother, see?'

Lefty relaxed his grip. Den's breathing eased.

'We shan't be in these parts long. Don't go worryin' about Edie. She can look after herself. In a little while, my pardners an' me, we shall have enough dinero to make us all rich, an' that includes you, Ma, Edie and everybody. So try an' look on the bright side, for once. Act like you have a future, an' maybe one day Ma will be proud of you!'

Lefty slapped him on the back, and Den made a great effort to look the way his brother expected him to be. In order to further ingratiate himself, he ticked off on his fingers the instructions as they had been given.

'Good for you, brother,' Lefty enthused, as he mounted up. 'I guess there's hopes for us Ferris boys, after all. Adios. Be seein' you in a day or two, Den. Say 'Hello' to Willie for me.'

As soon as they parted, Lefty backtracked into town, his eyes busy all the time. Den started towards the spot where the mule awaited him, but his forward momentum eased. He was thinking about Edie again. Presently he stopped walking, and sat down to rest.

16

Lefty Ferris did not like the idea of Teal having first got to the house where the money was thought to be secreted. He was a man who liked few people and only tolerated those with whom he had to associate. Although this was in the back of his mind from the time when he left his brother, Den, to make his own way clear of town, Lefty nevertheless moved cautiously on his return ride.

He made quite a big detour, and by the time he walked his pinto into the small tree stand at the back of the Strang house, he was perspiring with the effort of seeming ordinary, and avoiding the attentions of others. In a way, the fire which he had started with the explosive took the attention of the townsfolk away from strangers.

Standing in the timber, the homely-faced Ferris watched his chance before running across the open ground to the back door, where Teal admitted him.

'Any luck, amigo?' Lefty queried breathlessly.

Teal, who looked hot through his efforts since reaching the house, pushed back his hat and shook his head very decidedly. 'Not a glimmer of a clue,' he murmured. 'I've been over every room on the top floor, an' looked in all the obvious places that a man might hide things. No money. No notes an' no coin. There's a few dollars in coin in an ornament in the kitchen, but that's only for necessities. There's no sign of a fortune. I don't mind admitting I'm puzzled. Did you find your brother all right?'

'Oh, sure. I created a mild diversion, an' set him on the way to Red Rock. But let's get back to the important considerations. You say you made a careful check on everything upstairs?'

Lounging against a door frame, Teal gave his partner an odd look.

'When we're searching for a fortune,

can you imagine me bein' anything but careful?'

Left chuckled to try and smooth things over a little, but his mind was still calculating. He felt sure that Teal was not acting as though he had made a 'find' and was keeping it to himself. If the upstairs was 'clean', then probably the loot, if it was stashed in the house, was downstairs. He saw Teal watching him closely, and came to a decision.

'I know you won't take offence, Ross, if I suggest givin' the upper floor a second check? It sure is lucky there ain't no servant or anyone occupying the house, otherwise this little job would be rendered that much more difficult.'

Teal gestured for Lefty to go upstairs, and himself turned his attention to the room he was in. He concentrated on the furniture and the fireplace, and this time he used his knife to rip out upholstery where he thought something might be hidden. Lefty's heavy foot-steps thumping around upstairs showed that he was extremely busy. Every now and again there was extra noise which suggested that he had hurled a mattress onto the floor to further his search. On one occasion he sneezed.

Teal worked just as swiftly, and more quietly. Moreover, he was still watchful. From time to time he approached the window drapes and peered carefully in all directions to make sure that they were not about to be disturbed. All the time he was working, Teal's mind was busy. He was thinking back to the time when they first had Strang in their clutches, and when the talk had gone round to the prospects of ransom money. He remembered the exchanges, and who had said what. And gradually, from that moment of reasoning, his attitude towards the house as a hiding place changed.

He started his downstairs rounds once again, pulling down all the pictures and other wall decorations, studying the walls behind them and occasionally stripping a canvas from its frame, where there appeared to be a lot of padding.

Oblivious to the fact that he was destroying some very valuable treasures in his plundering quest, Teal gradually ran out of patience for his task. In the kitchen he had found a small store of factory-made cigarettes. He took them along with him, and seated himself at the foot of the staircase.

When the smoke from a cigarette was going down his throat, he leaned back his head and called up the stairs.

'Lefty, I've been thinking.' There was a slight pause, during which Lefty threw a padded chair against a wall and splintered it. The upstairs searcher then came into view, and sat on the top step. Teal resumed: 'I've been thinking about what Strang said when we had him there at the cabin. He said he'd never tell which part of his house his fortune was hidden in.'

Ferris had half-moons of perspiration under his armpits. He was breathing hard, after the way he had been searching. 'So?'

'So the loot may not be here in the house at all. Strang was the one to say it might be here. None of us said that. It's my belief he may have his money in the bank. If that's so, we're wastin' our time takin' this mausoleum to pieces.'

Lefty did not know for sure what a mausoleum was, but he gave out with a muted, half-strangled cry of rage. 'Why in tarnation didn't you let me beat the truth out of that — that moustached son of Satan, Ross? Always, you an' Willie know best. Could be that we shall lose a chance in a lifetime because I didn't exert a bit of pressure to find out exactly where to look!'

He thumped with his boot heels on the stair carpet and clenched his fists in pent-up rage.

'It may not be as bad as all that,' Teal called up to him. 'After all, the ransom note was the main way of extracting the money. Sooner or later, Strang's man or someone else will happen along there, an' then things will start to move. So what are we worryin' about? After all, we've been tryin' to make a fortune for a good few years now. A week or two longer won't age us all that much, will it?'

This time, Teal's soothing talk had no beneficial effect upon Ferris. The latter came storming down the stairs in a blind rage. Teal tactfully stepped aside and allowed his partner to make his way into the sitting-room. There Lefty crossed to the fireplace and picked up a heavy fire-iron. This he commenced to use on jugs and any sort of ornamental crockery which had survived Teal's search.

Teal expected his paroxysm to fade out in a minute or two, but this did not happen. Lefty aimed the metal rod at a huge fitted wall mirror and shattered it. His skittery laughter made Teal feel anxious. Before anything could be done to distract him, Lefty was aiming his weapon at the windows. He smashed one and knocked the glass out of a second one, while Teal protested in a voice which grew steadily louder. The steadier man was afraid that the noise would draw others to the house to find out what was going on.

Finally, he caught Lefty, who was trying to go past him, and grasped the fire-iron, which was held aloft in his hand. Largely due to the fact that there was an armchair close to them, Lefty managed to catch Teal off balance. The swarthy man lost his grip, and before he could get up off his knees Lefty had hit him a glancing blow on the head with the weapon.

Teal's head swam. He closed his eyes and gripped his head between his hands. Vaguely, he knew that Lefty was busily knocking out all the other panes of glass on the ground floor.

Lefty shouted: 'You laugh at me! Willie laughs at me. You all do it because I feel things more deeply than you do! You think I'm a fool! I'm no more unreliable than you! An' I'll prove it to you! I know how to finish off a job of work thoroughly. You'll see.'

There followed a couple of minutes of ominous quiet, while Lefty visited the kitchen. He came back with a big box of matches. A fixed wolfish grin bedevilled his features. He rasped the match into life and began to apply it to tinder-dry drapes, and anything that would burn.

A slight breeze was coming in through the holes in the window panes, and this helped the flames to spread with great rapidity. It was the steady crackle and the smell of smoke which finally helped Teal back to a full consciousness of what was happening.

'Lands sakes, Lefty, have you taken leave of your senses altogether? Do you want to announce to the whole world we're in here takin' the place apart?'

Teal moved slowly to his feet, watchful of his partner, as he was no longer sure how he would react to a direct appeal. The mounting heat along the front of the building as furniture and carpets caught fire, appeared to sober Ferris a little.

He backed off, chuckling fitfully, but the glazed look was leaving his eyes again. He peered at Teal as though he was not sure why the other had been on the ground.

'Hey, did I knock you over, Ross? Shucks, I'm sorry if I did. I guess I got a little too angry over this house of mystery. Why don't we get out of here before anyone asks us to explain what we're doing?'

Teal breathed out deeply, greatly relieved that Ferris' thoughts were lucid again. Together, they collected the things which they had walked in with, plus a few dollars from the kitchen, before leaving by the rear entrance and making their way to the copse where the horses awaited them.

As soon as they had their breath back, Teal remarked: 'I wonder if there really is a fortune in money in that place?'

'Would anybody know, other than

Strang, about a fortune like that?' Lefty wondered.

'If anyone else in town did, that man would be along here quite a bit before the fire-fighting equipment,' Teal pointed out, without fear of contradiction.

Lefty was nodding in full agreement. Already the first sightseers were arriving, running towards the front of the house.

★ ★ ★

By the time Slim's dun approached the southern side of town, the whole settlement was in a state of uproar. No one had seen such chaos in that part of the county since a hurricane came near to flattening everything in town fifteen years earlier.

Marshal Grain and his deputy, Garcia, were hunting through the buildings and open spaces, street by street, when Slim happened upon them. He reined in thankfully, pushed back his stetson and awaited an explanation as to what was happening.

The peace officers were quick to take a rest and to mop themselves, but slow to explain. While they were busy with their bandannas, Slim watched the mounting pall of smoke over the residential section. It hung over a fire of fairly vast proportions.

'You seem to have trouble here, Marshal,' Slim murmured. 'What caused the fire?'

'Nobody know that, but you should be interested. That's Jason Strang's place, and judgin' by the hold the fire has got on the buildin' there won't be much left to show when Mr Strang gets back there. By the way, have you seen him? Can you say when he'll be back home?'

'The answer is no to both your questions. Have you had any further developments in the Edith Lamont business?'

Grain leaned tiredly against an awning post. He glowered at Garcia,

246

who lowered his eyes while he gave the explanation. '*Señor*, it is as if the town is bewitched. Some fool started a fire with explosive. This drew us away from the peace office. While we were away, the prisoner, Ferris, escaped. Nobody saw him go. It is he we are lookin' for right now.

'The fire-fighters were slow to get to the Strang residence because they were still tired from fighting the other fire. Someone is here to make fools of us all.'

Garcia spread his thick arms in a helpless gesture. Slim found himself shaking his head, although he believed every small detail of what he had been told. Edith Lamont herself was the person concerned with Jason who had not had much prominence lately.

Could a mere woman have organised the escape of Den Ferris from the peace office and then set fire to the Strang residence? Slim felt reasonably sure that she could not have done it all on her own. His mind went back to the kidnapping of Jason. Apart from Jason himself, he — Slim — was the only man in town who knew about it. Unless, of course, the kidnappers had come along here to make more trouble.

He found himself saying: 'I must go along to Jason House and see what I can do to help.'

Grain and his assistant called out something about taking a hand themselves when they had finished their search. Slim wondered how the disappearance of Den would affect Jason's affairs. He supposed that the confession was still in the hands of the lawmen, and that it would stand up in court if the self-confessed forger remained at large.

17

Within less than an hour, the Strang residence would have to be written off as a total loss. While Slim was working his way across town, perspiring teams of manual workers were making lines and passing buckets of water forward, while other men worked the big manual pump which had to be hauled through the town by a team of four horses.

Few people had sympathy with the out-of-town owner of the building, but everyone was aware of the dangers of a fire spreading in a town where the houses and other buildings were largely fashioned out of wood. Several yards separated Jason House from the nearest neighbours on either side, but that did not prevent small groups of men from swarming over the roofs of the neighbouring dwellings and pouring water over the dry roof timbers and walls.

Flames were still roaring through the thick pall of smoke which hung like a seething mushroom over the burning shell of the doomed house. No one could get very close, and the hoses which were trained on it did not appear to make much difference to the fierceness of the blaze. Men shouted and changed positions in a weary automaton-like fashion. Those who could take no more of the arduous work on the pump, or in the bucket line, staggered to one side and clapped damp cloths to their heads and singed clothing.

Several scores of people were watching, but they were many yards away from the flickering flames and gusting smoke.

Slim left the frightened dun some fifty yards away from the scene of the fire. The crackle and roar was spellbinding for a human, let alone a frightened horse. The young detective began to push his way towards the front of the crowd which was hunched together in the open looking towards the frontage which was now wreathed in smoke. This was the sort of crowd where people did not mind giving way to a pushing sightseer. No one turned to find out who it was who so urgently wanted to be at the front.

In three minutes he was on the fringe of the crowd, not knowing why he had been so keen to get forward. Working in the bucket line might be helpful, but it would not further his investigations or his immediate and exacting commitments one little bit. For upwards of a minute he studied the doomed building and wondered what in particular Jason would regret having lost. Much of his furniture was of a smart exclusive style, but perhaps his pictures were the most valuable of his treasures.

He wondered what satisfaction a fire-raiser would get out of burning so many things of such value. It had not occurred to him that the fire, after all, might have started accidentally. Especially as it was the second fire in town that day.

As he brooded and hesitated over joining the fire-fighters, he found himself scanning the faces of the nearest watchers. He saw awe, fear and other emotions all mixed up in countenances of all ages, men and women alike. Fire had a compelling fascination for Westerners, as it had for countless generations of their ancestors.

His lungs were becoming accustomed to the hot air when another figure stumbled out of the line and zigzagged across the front of the watchers on unsteady legs. The face was smoke-blackened like most of the others, and yet there was something especially familiar about the figure and the unusual stance. The fellow pulled his singed hat off his head and revealed flattened strawcoloured hair.

Slim stared at him as though stunned. The fellow's breathing was noisy. His underlip was moving in and out due to the effort of respiration. He was a stockily-built man with a suggestion of a paunch and a slight stoop.

He was meandering towards the nearest pump, which was situated about ten yards beyond Slim, and about half that distance in front of the crowd of watchers. The man appeared to be all in.

Slim called to him. 'Hey, Den! Den Ferris, hold on a minute!'

It was easy to break away from the crowd and overtake the stunned fellow. Den had answered to his name, but his apparent apprehension could not have made him feel more desperate. He was too far gone physically. Slim put an arm round him and helped him as far as the pump. Flickering flames behind them at times highlighted their features. There was so much heat and smoke about that men forgot for a time that it was only mid-afternoon.

Slim propped Den against the side of the pump, keeping him out of the way of the muscular fellow who was operating the pump handle, and avoiding being trampled by those who came along with empty buckets for more water.

Scooping water out of the trough underneath the big tap, Slim contrived to refresh both of them. He had to shout to make himself heard by Den above the noise of the fire and its fighters.

'You decided to give yourself up for the forgin', Den?'

The cowed fellow merely nodded. Slim looked him over. Had he managed to escape unaided, or did he have allies in the town who had opened the doors as well as distracting the authorities by a fire alarm? Nothing was to be learned by a study of the tired face. At thirty, Den Ferris looked a wreck.

Slim shouted: 'This is Jason Strang's house! Did Edie set it on fire?'

Ferris' blank expression cleared up briefly. 'Nope, she didn't. Edie wouldn't do a thing like this. She's out of town some place, along South Creek Basin, workin' as a clerk to the ranchers out there. Mr Blake, you've got a bad opinion of a mighty fine young woman. She ain't the connivin' female you make her out to be! You hear?'

Slim nodded, and shouted again. 'I left Jason Strang at a shack known as Bobcat's Retreat, like I told you one time. But Jason has been taken away from there by force — he's been kidnapped! I can't help thinking this is another attempt to get a lot of money out of him by the same folks as before! Maybe Edie is tryin' kidnappin' now, for a change!'

'No, no, she wouldn't do that!' While Den was filling his lungs for another denial on Edie's behalf, something hit him in the chest, throwing him against Slim and making him gasp for breath. The stained printer's hands which clutched the left side of the chest were soon leaking blood. Den Ferris had been shot.

Slim lowered him as gently as possible to the ground; at the same time looking round to see who could have taken a potshot at him, and from where. It was all very bewildering, as the smoke was coming and going in long dense streamers in front of the house. The killer had excellent cover for his body, and also for the sound of his gun shot.

The same smoke which protected him, however, gave belated cover to the stricken man, and also to his questioner. Slim knelt beside Den, bending close in case he had anything of importance to say. His intelligence told him that this decrepit escaped prisoner was about to die.

'Tell me about the fire-raisers, Den,' Slim pleaded.

Ferris shook his head. He was protecting somebody, so it appeared, even in death. When he looked beyond speech, he gestured for Slim to come even closer. Into the detective's ear went the printer's last words.

'Look for Jason in Red Rock Canyon. Take care . . . '

The sound of his last breath rattling

in his throat was drowned by other noises. Slim put his hat over his face and left him there. He had other urgent business, with the living.

Working his way back through the crowd seemed to take a great deal of energy, but at last he had managed it. He went back to his mount and walked it to a livery which was devoid of human attention. There he gave it a thorough grooming and a light meal. Already he was contemplating a visit to Red Rock Canyon without waiting to acquire the ransom money.

Two things made him think he could do Jason some good by hurrying to the canyon. One hundred thousand dollars took a lot of getting together, even for a bank. So, presumably, the kidnappers ought to be prepared to wait for twenty-four hours. The other consideration appertained to a long-shot theory about the fire-raisers. If they were the same people as the kidnappers, he might be able to find Jason before they returned to the place where he was held captive.

This desperate situation called for desperate measures, even with Jason's life at risk.

★ ★ ★

Even while Slim was contemplating a return to Bobcat's Retreat and beyond, a man was dying a silent death amid rocks in the notorious box canyon. He died through a jagged throat wound.

When Jason Strang broke away from his captors and went deeper into the canyon, he was far from a defeated man. In fact, a part of his being rejoiced in the coming struggle for survival. He settled down behind rocks which backed onto a useful shallow stream of fresh water, and stayed there long enough to ascertain that his enemies would not prowl the canyon looking for him in darkness.

As soon as he was assured of this, he started to build himself a fire. This was comparatively easy, as he had with him matches and a knife which he had secreted about his person. Two small fishes caught in the stream ensured that he did not go to sleep hungry, and, while the fire warmed him, he contrived to fashion a weapon before he became too weary. A bow and an arrow. In using it, he would be gambling, because a bowman with only one arrow had to be a crack shot. He was undaunted, however, by the apparent odds against a successful escape from the canyon.

For a time, at least, his horse was beyond his reach, and nothing could be done to improve his lot. When the trio split their forces some hours later, this helped the beleaguered man in his desperate plan. He was close enough to know that some had departed, and he then began to position himself for an attack on the one man left to guard him.

During the morning hours, Willie Marvin was very watchful. It was in the early afternoon that his lonely task and the heat of the day began to dim his senses and make him sleepy. At first, his afternoon sleep was fitful, but soon his eyelids grew heavier and his head lolled upon his chest. This situation gave Jason a chance to perfect his hazardous plan.

A goodly number of yards away from Willie's camp, the trapped man climbed a tree. He had with him a collection of useful stones, his knife, and his hastily fashioned bow and arrow. His arrow was the item in which he took most pride. On three occasions he had changed the shaft for a better one. The feathers he had collected from the carcase of a dead bird. The barb was his masterpiece. It consisted of his favourite cravat stickpin, a miniature metal facsimile of a real arrow with a cunningly-wrought, sharp arrowhead barb of its own. This was lashed to the head of the arrow shaft and promised to do its function without spoiling the missile's flight.

High in the tree, he used his cravat as a sling to put stones close to the fire.

The first one was sufficient to rouse the dozing guard. Two subsequent ones had the effect of making Willie grin. He concluded that Jason, in desperation, was trying to make a fool of him with the stones. Taking up the challenge, Willie pulled his two revolvers and stepped clear of the rocks about the camp, walking slowly further into the canyon, and maintaining keen vigilance.

Two more stones hit ground on either side of him without his locating the source. He kept walking forward, but he stopped about every five yards as though to draw the opposition into making a give-away move. Jason's patience paid off. A short while before Willie got around to thinking about trees, Strang saw his target quite plainly through the foliage. He had his arrow already on the string. He sighted most carefully, released the shaft and grabbed for his knife and stones, in case he missed.

The arrow was aimed at Willie's chest. For most of its flight it appeared to be going too high to do him any damage. Moreover, the outlaw heard the slight sound which it made in flight. He tensed, looking around for it, but his actions could not forestall disaster.

The cunning barb ripped into his neck, severing an artery. He fought for several seconds against the onset of death, only to crumple on the spot before he had identified his killer's location.

18

At a distance, the most notable feature about Willie Marvin was his outsize stetson with the cartwheel brim. Lefty Ferris and Roscoe Teal saw the hat, and the head which was wearing it, over the top of a shoulder-high boulder near the camp where the trio had parted company.

They waved their hands in greeting, and received a return greeting quite promptly. What they did not expect was the sudden appearance of a shoulder weapon, and two accurate bullets, one aimed at each of them presumably by the man they had left in charge.

Jason was wearing Willie's hat. His shooting was accurate, but not sufficiently accurate to end the exchanges at that point. Lefty received a bullet burn on the outer side of his left upper arm, while Teal was more painfully wounded in the left side, above his hip bone.

Each rider was sufficiently used to tight situations to react swiftly. They plunged out of their saddles and promptly wriggled for the best rock cover that the canyon floor could afford them. While they were busily wriggling in, the man who had so surprised them disappeared from view.

It became clear after a short time lapse that he had gone deeper into the canyon. Gradually, it became clear to the two new arrivals that Strang had in some way bested Marvin, and used his hat to trick them. From time to time they called to one another as the situation became clearer.

Then, determined to be avenged upon their attacker, they advanced slowly into the canyon, fifty yards apart, armed with rifles as well as revolvers. Their wounds irked them, but years of campaigning over tricky terrain against cunning adversaries made them patient. After leaving town, they had moved swiftly back through Bobcat's land and into the canyon. Their speed had put them about a mile ahead of Slim, who was also heading the same way.

Around the time when Jason sprang his surprise, Slim was rapidly gaining on the outlaws, who were then half a mile ahead of him. The flurry of shooting gave the young detective some hope that Jason was alive, free and fighting back. Slim continued to overhaul the enemy, but he maintained all the caution he could muster.

As they advanced deeper into the canyon, so he followed them, a short interval later.

★ ★ ★

An hour after the pursuit into the canyon started, the outlaws were checking a creek near one cliff; also a small upstanding butte, a tree stand, and, near the other wall, a talus slope which looked to be a good hiding place. Slim, following them up, was headed more for the talus side than the creek.

All was quiet, though there was much tension felt by the opposing sides. A cunningly arranged man-made noise precipitated the end of the action. Two stones, so thrown that they focused attention on the butte, drew the attention of the outlaws to a flat, ledge-like shelf on the butte. By moving their position a few yards, they could see that the man in Marvin's hat was stretched out along the shelf, which to some extent overlooked them.

By signs and cautious whispers, Teal and Ferris outlined a stratagem to outwit the enemy. Ferris, whose left arm wound had spoiled him for revolver work, started to pump rifle shells towards the shelf where the figure was stretched out. At the same time, Teal broke cover and raced for the big rock, the top of which would give him a good shooting base from which to attack the butte.

Ferris continued to fire every few seconds, though the man he was aiming at did not return his fire. Teal broke cover, raced to the rock, and ran up it. As soon as he had reached the top, three successive rifle shots from an isolated stunted tree, which had never figured in the outlaws' calculations, riddled him and dropped him rather grotesquely to the canyon floor.

Seeing this, Ferris' control broke. He ran out of cover and raced for the foot of the butte. His swift move carried him ten yards before anyone could retaliate. Jason, in the tree, was having difficulty in lining up on him, but Slim, well placed in another direction, panned his Winchester with deadly accuracy and actually hit the running man with his second, third and fourth shots. So died the fratricidal Ferris.

The echoes of gunfire continued to reverberate around the canyon for quite a time after the shooting had finished. The corpse of Willie Marvin, wearing its own headgear, remained quite still upon the butte ledge, but from either side of the canyon Jason and Slim appeared and came together.

Both of them looked rather tired, and they were wet with perspiration, but there was no denying the look of triumph on both their countenances. Seated beside the gently moving canyon creek, they checked out each other's stories. Both proved to be good listeners.

★ ★ ★

About half an hour later Jason summed up. 'So, Den's confession is in the peace office, an' that clears me. It also incriminates Edith Lamont. Those jaspers fired my house, an' I don't like that. But anyways it's insured, an' there was no hidden money in it. I shan't need a town house again, because I'm goin' to buy the Box J back from the East Coast Cattle Company. I had a special option written into the deed of sale, and I've decided to be a man of action again, rather than a writer. That way, I can force men to respect me. Does this surprise you?'

Slim grinned broadly. 'Not very much. I've realised for a long time that you were a man of many parts, with a lot of resource. How you dealt with Marvin would make a good article write-up on its own. I'm curious to know what you'll do about Edie Lamont, though. At present she's out of town, workin' as a travellin' clerk to ranchers along the basin.'

Jason toyed with his moustache as he thought over the hardships which the young woman had caused him. At length, he came to a decision.

'I won't prosecute her, but if she stays in the district she'll have to show me proper respect and admit to my honesty. If she won't do that, I can make life mighty uncomfortable for her, and it won't help to have the sympathy of a lot of men, either.'

'I'm practically certain she won't give you any more trouble, Jason,' Slim opined. 'Why don't we backtrack to the cabin and make ourselves a meal there?'

Jason was a tidy man. He insisted on

burying the dead before leaving the canyon. He was also the one to round up the spare horses.

★　★　★

Two hours later, they parted outside the shack; Slim to return to town and inform the authorities of the latest happenings; Jason to remain in solitude for one more night, in order to compose two or three more articles before returning to town and to the life of a working rancher.

Slim returned to San Juan rather slowly and with mixed feelings. Mostly his thoughts were on Edie Lamont. She was a determined and attractive young woman. Even if she had intended to pass over her ill-gotten gains to one less fortunate than herself, she had still been too devious for his personal liking.

Slim was probably the only man in the district who had doubts about Den Ferris being the forger of the vital letter. He thought that Edie was clever enough to have forged it herself, and that Den was so fond of her that he could not let her take the blame.

Unless the young woman lost her nerve, her path and that of Jason Strang were likely to cross again. But she had gained little in her campaign against the orphan brought up by the Ferrises. Jason would continue to keep her at arm's length. Two Ferrises had died through her scheming.

Suddenly Slim threw back his head and yawned towards the sky. He was tired, and he knew that he had truly earned his pay on this current assignment. He looked forward to returning to Amarillo and Horace Danson with the news that Willie Marvin had died again.

We do hope that you have enjoyed reading this large print book.

Did you know that all of our titles are available for purchase?

We publish a wide range of high quality large print books including:
Romances, Mysteries, Classics
General Fiction
Non Fiction and Westerns

Special interest titles available in large print are:
The Little Oxford Dictionary
Music Book, Song Book
Hymn Book, Service Book

Also available from us courtesy of Oxford University Press:
Young Readers' Dictionary
(large print edition)
Young Readers' Thesaurus
(large print edition)

For further information or a free brochure, please contact us at:
Ulverscroft Large Print Books Ltd.,
The Green, Bradgate Road, Anstey,
Leicester, LE7 7FU, England.
Tel: (00 44) **0116 236 4325**
Fax: (00 44) **0116 234 0205**

NORTH FROM IDAHO

Jeff Sadler

The minute Anderson landed at the remote Idaho rail station, he knew he'd find trouble. Some people out there wanted him dead. They'd started with a bushwhacking at the station house, and when that didn't work they kept right on trying. Just like he knew they would. When he woke up in a funeral parlour after a saloon gunfight, Anderson thought it couldn't get much worse, but pretty soon he realized he was wrong. From Idaho the trail led north into the Canadian wilderness, where a bunch of outlaw killers waited . . .

KILLER BROTHERS

Bill Williams

Ben Gleason, nearing the end of a long prison sentence for killing his father's murderer, is told that his younger brother has been sentenced to hang in five days' time. In a desperate attempt to save his brother, Ben escapes and starts the long journey home. He faces danger and temptation before his journey ends in a tragic discovery. Instead of being reunited with his family and the woman he hoped to marry, Ben experiences a living nightmare. Soon, he may well face the hangman's noose himself.

Math Club

by Amy Ayers
Photographs by Gregg Andersen

Printed in Mexico

ISBN 13: 978-0-15-360221-4
ISBN 10: 0-15-360221-X

4 5 6 7 8 9 10 0908 16 15 14 13 12
4500361024

Harcourt
SCHOOL PUBLISHERS

The Math Club meets today.

Children come after school.
They play math games.

12

John has 12 counters.

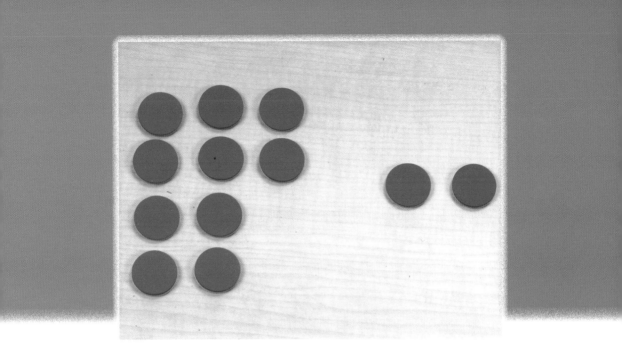

$$12 - 2 = 10$$

He takes away 2 counters.
Now he has 10 counters.

1

Jin draws 1 circle on the board.

1 + 2 = 3

She draws 2 more circles.
Now there are 3 circles.

7

Ann plays a counting game.
She has 7 stones.

$7 - 3 = 4$

Ann takes out 3 stones.
Now she has 4 stones.

4

Jack has 4 cubes on the table.

$4 + 2 = 6$

He gets 2 more cubes.
Now he has 6 cubes.

The children are busy.
They play and learn.

Soon they will hear a story.

They put away their games.

3

Amy played with flashcards.
She has 3 flashcards.

$$3 - 3 = 0$$

She puts away 3 flashcards.
Now 0 flashcards are left.

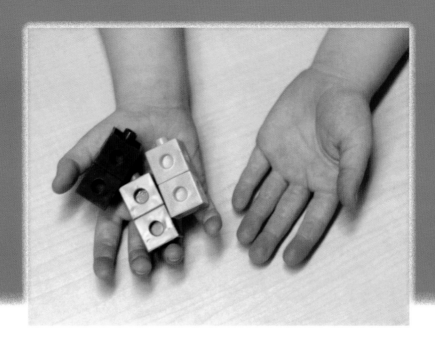

3

Rick picks up 3 game pieces.
He sees more pieces.

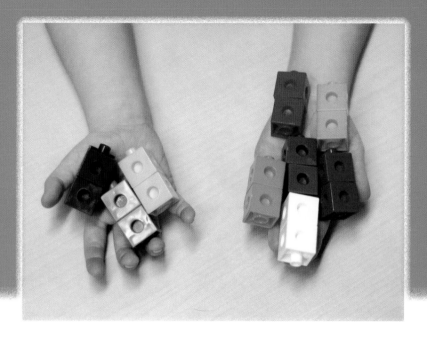

$$3 + 6 = 9$$

He picks up 6 more pieces.
Now he has 9 pieces.

0

The teacher is ready to read.
There are 0 children on the rug.

$$0 + 9 = 9$$

Now 9 children sit down.
They are ready to listen.

5

It is time to go home.
There are 5 coats.

$$5 - 2 = 3$$

Only 2 children take coats.
There are 3 coats left.

Everyone had fun at Math Club today.

They want to come again!

Glossary

club a group of people who meet to do something together

equals = $9 - 6 = 3$
9 minus 6 equals 3.

minus − $7 - 5 = 2$
7 minus 5 equals 2.

plus + $2 + 3 = 5$
2 plus 3 equals 5.